The
JETTY
CHRONICLES

Leonard Everett Fisher

MARSHALL CAVENDISH   New York

The JETTY CHRONICLES

Marshall Cavendish, 99 White Plains Road, Tarrytown, New York 10951-9001

The text of this book is set in 12 point Galliard
Printed in the United States of America   First edition
6 5 4 3 2 1

Library of Congress Cataloging-in-Publication Data
Fisher, Leonard Everett. The jetty chronicles/by Leonard Everett Fisher. p.   cm.
Summary: A boy describes growing up in the 1930s in a Brooklyn seaside
community filled with colorful characters.
ISBN 0-7614-5017-3   [1. Brooklyn (New York, N.Y.)—Fiction.] I. Title.
PZ7.F533Je   1997 [Fic]—dc21   97-6451   CIP   AC

In memory of my dear brother
RICHARD

AUTHOR'S NOTE

The social and environmental history of Lower New York Bay, as it unfolds in this work, are not extensions of my mind. All of the places, including the jetty, exist or did exist. For those of us who grew up within sight of the jetty, those rocks provided adventure, danger, dreams, and excitement. I took no liberties with the geography or geology of the area. What does comprise an extension of my mind, however, are the characters who weave in and out of this book. Imaginative and fictional, they are within the context of realism to which they are laced. They do belong to me. They are composites of people who touched my life. My brother was real enough.

All the events depicted herein happened. I confess to some rearrangements for the sake of fiction.

LEF
Westport, CT

A life on the ocean wave,
        A home on the rolling deep;
Where the scattered waters rave,
        And the winds their revels keep!
Like an Eagle caged I pine
        On this dull unchanging shore:
Oh, give me the flashing brine,
        The spray and the tempest roar!
                —Epes Sargent

from *A Life on the Ocean Wave*

In the Beginning ————

When I was a schoolboy, I spent endless hours on the end of a slippery, sea-mossy jetty that poked into Lower New York Bay. Like a giant finger, the one-hundred-fifty-foot-long man-made pile of rocks—"rocks"—that's what the locals called the jetty— "rocks"—pointed due west from Brooklyn to Staten Island, some three or four miles away. Swinburne and Hoffman Islands, whose presence in the Lower Bay is hardly a footnote in the history and mythology of New York, lay in between. Yet, here on these flat and desolate islands stood hospitals for very contagious and infectious diseases. And here, on these islands, ailing immigrants suspected of having the plague or some incurable malady were confined to quarantine hospitals, having been removed from the ships that brought them to these American shores. Incurables were either returned to their homelands or died there. Those who were miraculously cured were admitted to the United States. All that was a hundred years ago.

During World War II, Hoffman Island was the western anchor of a submarine net and minefield that blocked the entrance to New York Harbor. Ships had to have proper identification to enter the harbor through the net. A gunboat swung a gate back and forth allowing ships to enter or leave. The eastern anchor of the net and minefield was the jetty. Nothing much seemed to happen on Swinburne Island. Swinburne was a mystery to my younger brother, Richard, and me, and all of our friends. The prevailing opinion was that the island was the site of a horse graveyard and glue factory. Horses had disappeared altogether too quickly from the streets of New York's five boroughs. They had been too speedily replaced by autos and trucks with "horsepower" in their engines. Everyone living near the jetty and within sight of Swinburne was sure that the horses were turned into glue on the island.

Our house was about fifty yards from the jetty. Nothing stood between us and Staten Island but the jetty, the Atlantic Ocean to our left, and Gravesend Bay to our right. We lived on Norton's Point with a clear and unobstructed front porch view of all that passed in and out of New York by water. A block away was the Norton's Point Lighthouse.

The place itself was Sea Gate, a tiny, mile-square enclave on the edge of southwestern Brooklyn. To most outsiders, distant, sleepy Sea Gate—the "Gate" to insiders—was beyond the outer reaches of the real world. It was a Brigadoon—a magical place where people awoke from their gray winter slumber each year on or about Memorial Day to play and sunbathe on the wide, seductive beaches until Labor Day. The hibernation began the day after Labor Day and deepened during the damp, lonely winter until the population was comatose. Memorial Day came none too soon.

That was a long time ago. Now the jetty is almost gone, a victim of the relentless sea. It has sunk nearly out of sight, invisible at high tide, hardly visible at low tide. Originally installed in 1907 to prevent the erosion of a small pleasant beach and the shore beyond, the jetty's work was weakened by a series of terrible storms and the changing geology of the region. Even the beach is gone.

During August and September when bottom-feeding fluke ran strongly with the incoming tide, chased by bigger fish, the far end of the jetty became crowded with fishermen. The ticket of admission out there was a flawless overhand casting technique. There was no other way to get your line into the water safely away from the rocks and clinging seaweed without fouling all the other lines. A sidearm caster was dangerous. Anyone casting a line sidearm was more apt to hook a fellow fisherman than a fish. A "sidearmer" could also whip his neighbor into the water with his rod. The rods we used were not today's lightweight, slender, flexible, plastic poles. They were well-varnished chunky hardwood "boat poles." They did not bend. There was no getting around it, sidearmers were an unwelcomed lot.

I gave up fishing off the jetty when the war came. I gave my fishing gear to my younger brother, Rich, and joined the army. No one was allowed out on the jetty, anyway, or on the beach for that matter. The whole place was patrolled by the military. They not only watched over the submarine net from a pillbox built just a few feet away from our front lawn, they also mounted cannons all along the beach to guard against an invasion. None of those soldiers could skim a *Venus Mercenaria*—a clamshell, that is— thirty-five yards across the water with four or five skips the way I could. You had to hold the shell in a certain way and fling it with an underhand-sidearm pitch.

Rich was a more successful fisherman than I was. He could attach four hooks on long leaders to one line and come up with four fish at once. Somehow, those fat and slimy, purply, softly barbed sandworms we used for bait and which we yanked bare-handed from the salty ooze of the breakwater lagoon, worked more miracles for Rich than they did for me. There were other types of bait—shiners and killies, pork rind and tinfoil—we could have used and did use once in a while. But Rich and I were barefoot traditionalists who preferred worms above all else.

Most of the sensible fishermen who jostled each other for favorable positions were gone by high tide. Those who remained— usually one or two newcomers who did not know any better—ran the risk of being stranded, soaked, splintered, or submerged. At least half the jetty would disappear under the rolling sea. Only the rocks at the very end would remain high, out of the water but damp. They could not escape the wash and spray of the Atlantic Ocean.

When the moon was full not even the rocks at the jetty's end were visible. The rocks went under, totally hidden by the spring tide caused by the moon's gravitational pull. When the tide ebbed under the full moon, the neap tide exposed every rock of the jetty high and dry above its sandy foundation.

Fog kept reasonable people off the jetty. I never went out there in a fog. If I could not see the end of the jetty from its foot on the beach, a distance of one hundred and fifty feet, I did not venture out on it. The flat, metallic *bong* that issued from the fog bell of the Norton's Point Lighthouse was ample warning. The sound of it floating through the misty shroud that hid the sea seemed always to be a signal of doom.

None of us locals were conscious of the sounds of the sea— the various bells, horns, wildlife. Most of all we were deaf to the constant, rhythmical beat of the breakers as they rolled into the beach, snapping against the rocks and crashing into the seawall, a ten-foot-high United States Government wood and concrete barrier that separated the ocean from most front yards. Yet, we all heard the fog bell. It was the sound of eternity.

One foggy, wintry night in 1947, a year after I had left the army, we were all suddenly jarred loose from our beds. It happened to have been New Year's Day about an hour or two before dawn. The jolt was so explosive it sent shock waves through the house. Looking out the bedroom window I could see the massive bow of a twelve-thousand-ton "liberty ship," the *Charles E. Mason,* soaring out of the fog. I could almost touch it. House lights from all around—punctuated by the red beacon of the lighthouse as it rotated once every twenty or thirty seconds—threw an eerie halo around the ship's looming bow.

A veteran of four wartime ocean crossings, one of which was in a leaky "liberty," the *Isaac Mayer Wise,* I knew exactly what I was looking at. This liberty had run aground on the jetty at low tide during a very foggy night of celebration. An accordion, laughter, and singing had been drifting through the fog all night long as we celebrated the new year on land.

The bow of the *Charles E. Mason* had practically gone through the bedroom window. The bridge and forward superstructure appeared to undulate in and out of the drifting mist. The rest of the ship lay hidden in the heavy fog and night. The eerie look of the scene was heightened by a flashlight from some invisible section behind the bridge as it came forward through the gloom. A lone figure holding the flashlight leaned over a railing to assess the situation. A voice cried out from somewhere along the bridge.

"Where are we, Mr. Swanson?" Back came the reply, "On the rocks, Captain."

It took four days and two United States Navy oceangoing tugs to drag the monster off the jetty and restore an unobstructed seascape. The ship had hit the bottom with such force that she drove up onto the jetty and slid along the rocks and beach until she hit the seawall.

15

But those rocks, that jetty, would not be intimidated by twenty-six million pounds of iron and steel on its way to being scrapped. Strangely, not a rock was dislocated—scratched and roughed up—but not dislocated. When the tugs finally pulled her free, only strips of the jetty's moss, seaweed, mussels, and barnacles went with her.

I sat on those rocks in daylight and at low tide as often as I could to watch the world sail by two and a half miles away. And two and a half miles' distance straight out on the water was like viewing something at the end of one's outstretched arm. I grew up watching the comings and goings of every great ship in the world. I tracked the fish, birds, weather, currents, and people, let alone the flotsam and jetsam of the ever-rolling tidal sea. Those unyielding rocks were my transport to life.

1934 ————————————————

Late one July afternoon in 1934, I scrambled out to the jetty's end only to find my favorite rock occupied by a bony old man with a wind-tossed shock of white hair. The old man was sitting comfortably cross-legged on a green and grainy rock looking out at the empty sea. He paid no attention to me. I found another green and grainy rock for my perch, a little put out that my "seat" had been taken.

"You're sitting on Manhattan schist," the old man volunteered, still looking out at the sea. "And if you are wondering if we know each other," he offered, still not looking at me, "I can save you the trouble. The answer is no! And you are still sitting on Manhattan schist."

It had been a rare clear and breezy day for July. Now the faint odor of salt and fish lingered on a diminishing wind. The sun, falling in the western sky, delivered its usual blinding glare to the water. The white light on the calm sea jumped and flickered on the gently moving surface. It was too blinding to look at. We shielded our eyes from the sparkling glare. A crab scooted out of a dark, rocky hollow. It crawled between us and finally disappeared into another dark, rocky hollow.

I looked at the old man. I had never seen him before. I had

no idea who he was. Probably someone's grandfather.

"Manhattan schist?"

"That's right, my boy. There's Inwood dolomite—that's a pink marble—Fordham gneiss, and Manhattan schist. This is Manhattan schist. The whole island of Manhattan over there," he said, pointing northward beyond Gravesend Bay, "is made up of those three rocks."

"How do you know?" I demanded. I was more than vaguely interested. I had been to Manhattan a few times.

"How do I know?" he replied. "Why! I helped build the BMT. You do know what the BMT is, do you not?"

"Of course I do! Who doesn't! It's the subway. *The Brooklyn-Manhattan Transit.*" There! That got him. Not bad for a twelve-year-old kid.

"Do you know what a geologist is?" he queried.

"No."

"Of course not. Who does? A geologist studies rocks. Well, never mind. Just let's say that I know my rocks. These boulders," he insisted, "were dynamited out of the earth to make a tunnel for the BMT. That took some doing, you know."

"Is that so?" was all I could muster. I hated the BMT! It never failed to give me a round-trip headache from Coney Island's Stillwell Avenue Station to Manhattan and back. I was sorry that there was so intimate a connection between the BMT and the jetty.

"When was that?" I added, not knowing what else to ask, sensing that the old man wanted me to ask something.

"Nineteen ought seven. Twenty seven years ago. Nineteen ought seven," he repeated. "That's when the BMT opened."

It was hard for me to imagine that anything but my mother,

father, grandparents, and dinosaurs were alive and stalking the earth at that time.

"That was long before you were around, young fellow. But fear not. These rocks are a lot older than that. In fact, they are a good deal older than I am. Believe it or not!"

I assumed that both man and rocks were old. Which one was older was irrelevant, academic, and not very significant.

"Well, let me tell you, my boy. This stuff is Precambrian. That makes it at least a billion years old. And that was . . ."

I could not hear the rest. Several blasts of a rich and deep ship's horn overwhelmed the old man's voice. The sound echoed all around the bay. The old man kept on talking just the same. His mouth moved. His face was animated. He pointed to this rock and that rock. He might just as well have been an actor in a silent film. Not a sound he made could be heard above the horn.

Thinking that the great blasts had come from a liner departing New York with a final salute as was sometimes done, I looked toward the Narrows, that slender channel separating the harbor from the open sea and Brooklyn from Staten Island. Nothing. Another series of blasts. Then a single blast and there she was, gliding out of the blinding reflection on the water and slowly moving toward the Narrows. Beyond, and out of sight, were the Statue of Liberty, the Hudson River, and the ship's berth.

"I tell you, my boy," the old man began to shout.

"That's the *Bremen*," I interrupted.

The old man looked up to see the huge German ship slowly drift past Hoffman Island. "The Precambrian period," he persisted despite the arrival of the *Bremen*, "was . . ."

"That's the *Bremen*, all right," I maintained. "And she probably just set a new world speed record. She's very fast. She did about twenty-eight knots when she broke the record the first time. Let's see, that would be about thirty-two miles an hour. Wow! I bet she just did thirty knots even!"

"How do you know that ship out there is the *Bremen*," the old man challenged, "and not the *Europa* or the *Berengaria* or the *Mauretania*?"

Whoops. I had to watch my step. It sounded as if the old man knew as much about ships as he did about rocks.

"Oh, that's easy. The *Berengaria* and the *Mauretania* are Cunard liners—English. Cunards have black and red smoke-stacks—black on top, red on the bottom—a little more red than black. French ships have red and black funnels, too," I added, changing "smokestack" to "funnel" for better effect. It sounded more nautical. "French funnels may look like English funnels—but they are different. The black and red are evenly divided."

"That still does not explain that ship out there!"

"That's easy enough, too. The *Berengaria* has three stacks. The *Mauretania* has four stacks. The English stacks are tall and narrow. That ship over there has only two very stubby stacks."

"Is that so?"

"The *Bremen* and the *Europa* are sister ships," I lectured with growing confidence. "They are North German–Lloyd liners—German! They ride low in the water and have two short tan stacks like that one over there."

The big ship was now passing Fort Wadsworth on the Staten Island shore and slowly nosing her way into the Narrows.

"I bet you didn't know that the *Berengaria* was once a German ship, too—Hamburg-American Line. The English grabbed her after Germany surrendered. The *Mauretania* was the *Lusitania*'s sister ship. You know, the one that was sunk by a German sub.

20

Maybe that's why the English grabbed the *Berengaria*." I figured all this information would impress him and improve my stature.

"Remarkable!" the old man exclaimed. "Remarkable! But you still have not told me why the ship out there is the *Bremen* as you say it is, and not the *Europa* as it could very well be."

Now I had him. "Because the *Europa* was taken out of the Transatlantic Service temporarily. I read that in the papers. And because that one out there has big white letters on her bow that spell B-R-E-M-E-N!"

The old man grunted, turned his back to the water, and pointed to the beach. "In the beginning, all of this Manhattan schist was probably just like the sand on the beach." He waved his arm like a wand. "It wasn't as fine, perhaps. A bit more granular. Nevertheless it was sand."

How do you like that! The old guy showed not the least interest in the *Bremen* or in what I knew. He indulged me briefly and then turned to his own obsession, the rocks, a larger scheme of life and history. Only the rocks seemed to matter. He was caught up in the Manhattan schist and refused to let go. He was going to rave on about the jetty's composition no matter what. The *Bremen*, which happened to be the world's fastest ship, a real queen of speed, was now dead in the water off the quarantine station and being inspected by United States Public Health officers looking for some dreaded disease.

"I bet she's got a case or two of typhoid or yellow fever on board," I mused loudly. "Maybe even smallpox or the bubonic plague." I was deliberately trying to distract the old man and turn the conversation my way again. But he did not care about the water or anything on it, at least not then. His passion was for the rocks.

The sun had dropped a little lower in the cloudless sky. It was centered ahead of us and turning orange. Soon it would glow a bright crimson with the promise of thick summer heat tomorrow. The water, now tinged with a streak of the sun's fire, had become flat and quiet. Much of the blinding glare was gone. Gone, too, was the *Bremen*. There were no awful diseases on board. She had disappeared into Upper New York Bay, into the harbor, where waiting tugs nudged her great bulk carefully into a Hudson River berth. There was no breeze. The air had become still, motionless, and very warm. Nothing moved on the water. It was as if the world had stopped, and the old man and I were adrift on a magical vessel.

Swinburne and Hoffman Islands were silhouetted against the smoky blue-violet hills of Staten Island. They seemed more mysterious than ever as they appeared to float on the gathering haze. The stillness that descended over us was haunting. Not even the gulls, wheeling overhead, squawked their usual shrill complaint. The only sound was the gentle surge of the sea finding weedy, barnacled crevices among the rocks and trickling out again.

The old man looked sadly at the water. In that moment, he, too, was being transported elsewhere, captured by the calm, and muttering to himself:

> "All in a hot and copper sky
> The bloody sun at noon,
> Right above the mast did stand,
> No bigger than the moon."

"Did you say something?" I asked.

"Coleridge," he replied and went on muttering:

"Day after day, day after day,
We stuck, nor breath nor motion;
As idle as painted ship
Upon a painted Ocean."

I had no idea then that the old man's soft incantation about the sea was some verses from my father's favorite poem, the *Rime of the Ancient Mariner*, written long before anyone thought of blasting a subway tunnel under Manhattan and depositing some of its rocks on Norton's Point. But while I understood not a mumble, I had an idea that it had less to do with Manhattan schist and more to do with the stillness that had enveloped us—the stillness of early evening and the changing tides.

I waited for more verses. There were no more. The old man turned back to stare at the beach and the seawall aflame in the light of the plummeting crimson sun.

I glanced at the tide pole some five hundred yards to our left. It was anchored just about where Lower New York Bay ran into the Atlantic Ocean. It was all the same water to me, blue-gray and rougher on the Atlantic side, green-gray and calmer on the bay side. The tide pole had begun to lean seaward, a sure sign that the tide was "coming in," rising. It would take another hour or two before parts of the jetty would become flooded and the black of night would make it a dangerous roost for humans, fit only for seagulls. Dinnertime was not far off. But neither I nor the old man was in any rush to leave the rocks.

As was usually the case with an incoming tide, the traffic on the sea-lanes and channels leading into the harbor began to pick up. The outgoing tide always generated traffic in the opposite direction: out to sea. To Europe, Africa, Asia, South America, and distant points everywhere in the world.

Steaming in front of me in the fading light—the old man might just as well not have been there as he brooded with his back to the sea—was a small rusty freighter flying a white flag with a red ball in its center. She was Japanese and a long way from home. The ship was riding high, her waterline many feet above the surface. She was arriving in New York without a cargo, or at the very least, with an extremely light load. A full load would have set her deeply in the water.

Usually, I could read the names on the ships if the letters were large and clear enough. I was able to read the *Bremen* easily. But this ship was such a rusty bucket that all I could pick out was the second part of what was a two-part name I knew: M-A-R-U.

Not far behind the *Shigamitsu Maru* was a string of oil tankers riding low and heavy in the water, straining to reach the Bayonne refineries in New Jersey across the Upper Bay from Brooklyn. The blistering sun was backlighting the traffic, making it difficult to identify the ships. The only thing I could tell from their silhouettes was that they were all silently heading for New York on the incoming tide.

"Do you see all that stuff sparkling in the rocks?"

The old man was at it again. He had broken the spell. Everything was coming alive again. I heard the swish of water hissing and gurgling into and past the jetty. I could hear the distant throb of a ship's engine, something I was not aware of before. Another ship sounded off. And still another answered with a blast of its own. A seagull gliding lazily overhead suddenly shrieked and dived straight into the water. A brief splash and the bird was back in the air, a small fish struggling in its beak. Within seconds there were a dozen other gulls diving for their supper. A school of shiners had invaded the area.

The sun still had not set. It hung in the sky, a red ball of fire, seemingly motionless, unwilling to disappear behind the Staten Island landscape. And in that eternity of suspended time, the Gravesend Bay baitmen appeared.

Two crusty rowboats were easily and steadily rowed each by a lone oarsman in overalls facing forward as he pushed the oars. Quickly they passed the tip of the jetty, cast their nets into the school of shiners, and deprived the gulls, whom the boatmen had been watching, of their evening meal.

"Well, do you see all that sparkly stuff?" the old man repeated.

I looked at the bits of shiny material that speckled the rocks. It was not something I had never noticed before. Some people called it "mica." My father liked to call it "isenglass." I had no idea why. Isenglass sounded German or Dutch or something like that. My father was neither. He was born on a farm near Canarsie Creek, when Brooklyn was an independent city. Now it was incorporated into the City of New York as one of five boroughs.

"There's a lot of quartz and bits of garnet in schist," the old man continued. "And a fair sprinkling of 'muscovite' and 'biotite.'"

"Muscovite? Biotite?" I knew what quartz was. And somewhere I had read, probably in the encyclopedia, that garnet was a reddish glassy gemstone. But "muscovite"? "biotite"? These were strange names.

"I bet you never heard of muscovite and biotite," the old man declared.

"Nope."

"How about 'isenglass'? Did you ever hear of isenglass?"

"Yup."

"How about mica?"

Now I began to make a connection between isenglass, mica,

muscovite, biotite, and the shiny stuff in the rocks. "Yup," I shot back with considerable annoyance and impatience. It was time to get off the rocks. But he was in no hurry.

"Well, good," he responded with genuine delight. " 'Mica' or 'isenglass' or whatever you want to call it is a flaky, glassy stuff that comes in two varieties: white or colorless—that would be your muscovite; black would be your biotite." With that he pried some of each loose with a penknife from the rock he was sitting on. He handed the chips to me in the hope that I might begin "an important mineral collection."

The sun started to descend again. Its bottom edge now touched the Staten Island hills. Soon it would sink behind the hills and bring on the night. Four of the men from the two rowboats—the netters—were on the beach hauling in their nets. The boats with their rowers drifted quietly off shore. The gulls squawked angrily as thousands of tasty shiners wiggled into the nets to be sold the next day for bait.

The sun was gone now. The sky above us turned a deep purple-green. It glowed orange, red, and violet where the sun had disappeared. It would not be total blackness for a while. But the tide was rising quickly. A sudden wave smashed into one of the lower rocks and soaked us with its salty spray. It was time to go home.

We began to pick our way along the jetty toward the beach. I knew an easy route and led the way. I looked back from time to time to make sure the old man hadn't slipped and fallen into the water. He was still there, all right, prattling on about sand.

"Sand," he yelled. "That's all it ever was. Sand. A billion years of pressure turned sand into schist. And all these sparkly bits you see in the rocks are probably from the original sand. A billion years old. Can you imagine that?"

No. I could not imagine that. And if he did not stop raving on, he was never going to make the beach. I could not imagine a billion years, anyway. Old was anything—people, rocks, it made no difference—that was around before I was born, even the day before I was born.

"What about Brooklyn?" I asked him as we climbed down from the last rock and stood on the beach. "What about Sea Gate? What are they made of?"

"Sand," the old man replied. He kneeled to retie a lace on his sneaker. "Just plain sand."

"Will it become schist like the jetty—like Manhattan?"

"Maybe. But probably no."

"How come?"

"The sea will wash it all away and cover the earth one day before any of that can happen."

That was the most ridiculous thing I had ever heard. All this and the jetty, too! Covered by the sea! Impossible. *That will never happen,* I thought as we climbed the rickety iron ladder to the top of the seawall.

"I'll tell you something else, young fellow. If the Germans or anyone else keep building ships like your *Bremen* and fill the ocean full of them—and mark my word, they'll do just that—there won't be any sand left here to worry about, or a Sea Gate, or even a Brooklyn. And that jetty behind us will drown in the deluge."

"I don't get it," I said.

"Let me put it this way. I know all about your *Bremen.*" The old man kept insisting that the ship belonged to me. "Your *Bremen,*" he snapped, continuing the lecture that began out on the end of the jetty. "I happened to be on the main beach further down when the *Bremen* broke the *Mauretania*'s speed record and won the

Transatlantic Blue Ribbon. That was back in July '29, I think. We all knew she was coming in. There were a hundred people on the beach when we spotted her on the horizon. As she came off Sandy Hook she was trailed by a steam of smoke from her stacks ten miles long. She was coming so fast and so bent on breaking the record that she never bothered to stop at Ambrose Lightship to pick up a harbor pilot. But on she came passing us at full speed.

"And then we saw it. At first we thought it was just her wake. But that 'wake' rose and rose and rose. It was a mountain of water heading toward us with unbelievable speed and power—a tidal wave set up by the ship's propellers rotating at full speed. In minutes and without warning that wave struck along the entire half mile of beach sweeping the sand a hundred yards inland. It flattened anyone standing in its path. Luckily no one was in the water swimming or else they would have drowned. Some people were hurt, however. No one was killed, thank heavens. That wave traveled a good five miles before it hit us. And when it receded it not only took some clothing, pails and shovels, chairs, umbrellas, and blankets, it also took some of the sandy beach, too. Ever since then, these ships have become too numerous. Each one tries to outdo the other while the beaches around here have been getting narrower and narrower. Someday someone is going to drown in one of those waves and then the lawmakers will pass a law to slow those liners down as they enter harbor waters.

"Of course, there is always a certain amount of natural erosion. Ordinary wave action picks away at the beach, too. That's why the jetty was put there in the first place, to save this little beach. But I tell you, my boy, in the end, it will not matter. The North Pole ice cap will melt. The oceans will rise and drown us all."

When I asked the old man when all this would happen, he

muttered, "In about a million years!" I quit worrying right then and there. But the old man was way off his mark. "A million years," he said. Wrong! In less than fifty years the jetty and the beach would be gone! Now that's something to worry about!

I climbed the front porch steps and took another look at the jetty. The old man faded into the leafy shadows of Beach 48th Street. I still had no idea who he was. But then again, I did not know everyone in Sea Gate. I saw him one more time a couple of weeks later prowling along the seawall. It was drizzling and he was looking down at the waves slicing along the wall unmindful of the rain. I did not leave the porch to talk to him and he did not see me. I never did find out his name or who he was. When we parted company he reminded me to "look up" *geology* in the dictionary. "That's spelled G-E-O-L-O-G-Y. It's a very useful science."

The night had come. A few lights twinkled across the bay on Staten Island's South Beach. The tide ran high under a three-quarter moon. A steady rhythm of waves rolled up onto the little beach and pounded the jetty.

"Where have you been?" my worried mother queried. "Didn't you hear me calling? Don't tell me. You've been on the jetty again. Well, you're too late for dinner. We've all eaten. You'll just have to fend for yourself. How many times have we told you . . ."

1935

I didn't know Horace Monash all that well. He was just a nodding acquaintance. And Horace knew me as the kid who lived in the sprawling house overlooking the jetty. Horace Monash, thirtyish, and a reasonably good-looking bachelor, had no time for me, barely a teenager.

Horace was one of the "summer people," an alien race living temporarily among the "all-year-rounders." Horace arrived on the Fourth of July this hot summer of 1935, and would be gone by Labor Day. Summer people were never encouraged by the all-year-rounders to become too friendly. Outsiders forever, they were tolerated as long as they obeyed the local laws, paid their rents or taxes, and cut their lawns once a week, preferably late Friday afternoon but no later than Saturday morning.

Horace didn't have to worry about cutting any grass. He lived in a furnished room in an old, well-kept, and elegant Victorian house called the "White House." It was a gleaming white building not far from the jetty. On weekends, he sunned his muscular body and exercised on a large flat rock at the foot of the jetty. Lucky for him it was an unusually dry summer. The sun seemed to shine everyday, especially on Saturdays and Sundays.

During the week, Horace took the scruffy-looking, tired, old iron steamboat, *Mayflower*, at the Sea Gate pier on Gravesend Bay to Battery Park in Manhattan. From there, most of the boat commuters took the BMT subway to work. Horace had few friends on the *Mayflower* and lost himself in the crowd. No one knew where Horace went once he walked off the boat.

Eventually, the *Mayflower* was replaced by the *Sylph,* a smaller, faster, sleeker boat with a questionable career. She had been a rumrunner in the employ of bootlegging gangsters during the thirteen years of Prohibition. The *Sylph* went straight in 1933 when Prohibition was repealed and it was legal to make, sell, buy, and drink whiskey again. Her former owners were still in prison, however, "up the river" in Sing Sing. They were caught checking their competitor's illegal inventory of scotch whiskey in a Brooklyn garage. While it wasn't exactly illegal to check their competitor's inventory, it was illegal to shoot them first. Their competitors were dead at their feet, riddled with Thompson submachine gun bullets.

None of this had any connection with Horace Monash. He was long gone from Sea Gate and the jetty when the *Mayflower* blew her final, farewell whistle. During that hot and innocent summer, Horace always appeared at the jetty with a girlfriend. There seemed to be three or four of these ladies who rotated their company with him. And while Horace never turned up with the same woman twice in a row, he always wore the same expensive blue silk beach robe trimmed with red piping. If HORACE MONASH hadn't been emblazoned on the back, in white, like a billboard or a prizefighter's robe, it would have been more appropriate in a boudoir rather than at the shore. Except for one other small detail, Horace would have gone unnoticed. Sewn to the left breast pocket of his robe was a very official-looking red, white, and blue emblem that seemed to be the authentic Olympic Games shield. The same shield was sewn to the right leg of Horace's dazzling white swimming trunks.

Rumor had it that Horace Monash was a long-distance swimmer training for the Olympic games to be held in Germany the next year, 1936. Rumor insisted that Horace was scheduled to swim a 350-mile length of the 800-mile-long Rhine River! It was a little known fact that Horace himself had started the rumor in a purposeful offhand conversation with his landlady. The rumor reached each of Horace's lady friends. It worked! They were impressed beyond reason with his manliness and courage. That was the limit of Horace Monash's intent: to impress the ladies. Of course, there were those who scoffed at the whole idea of Horace's notoriety.

My father was one of these. "Good Lord!" he exclaimed when I tried to convince him that Horace was indeed for real. "Look at the insignia," I begged, "doesn't that tell the story?"

"Listen," my dad went on, "it took Gertrude Ederle a half day to swim twenty-six miles across the English Channel. It's going to take that fellow Monash a month to swim the Rhine provided he lives to see the finish line. Besides, if he is in training as all you muddleheads around here seem to think, where are his coaches?"

"Nonsense," interrupted a neighbor. "No one who looks like Horace can not be in the Olympics. He's an Olympian!"

"So. Let him take an extra week. Let him take an extra two weeks," another added. "It will not matter. He'll be the only survivor and win the gold medal. America wins every time. America will show the world!"

Lately there were hints of dark doing inside Germany. A peculiar, posturing fellow with a mustache was running things. He and his associates all wore brown uniforms with armbands. Eighteen years had passed since Germany had been driven to her knees in World War I. This fellow, Adolf Hitler, had made a few menacing speeches and now Germany was no longer on her knees.

Gradually the jetty crowd began to look at Horace Monash as a symbol of American courage, strength, and goodness. Horace responded in kind. He would remove his glorious red, white, and blue beach robe with the flourish of a preening matinee idol. He would ceremoniously hand it to whichever lady friend was his at the moment. Under Horace's haughty gaze she would carefully fold it and set it down softly on a smooth blanket. Horace would then permit his lady to remove his sneakers and set these down on the blanket with loving care. Horace would then walk a couple of yards up and down to reveal his big, bronze, loosely muscled swimmer's body to his companion and everyone else on the seawall above. The crowd watched with admiration. Some wondered.

Horace's greatest admirer, through it all, was the attractive girl he'd have along. She would rub him with suntan lotion, and send him trotting off toward the water with a gentle shove.

But Horace never ventured out to a depth beyond his knees. There he would stand in knee-deep water, arms akimbo, rhythmically twisting this way and that. Finally, he would reach into the water, splash himself tenderly, making certain not to damage his well-coiffed wavy brown hair, and head for the flat rock at the foot of the jetty. There he would lie, turning every so often to fry in the sun evenly.

His girlfriend sat quietly at his feet reading and waiting. A half hour of this and Horace would ceremoniously rise to do calisthenics—first on the flat rock, then on the sand at the water's edge. Once he interrupted his routine to give a couple of kids his autograph, sending them on their way up the seawall ladder with a friendly pat on their rumps.

There was no doubt any longer. Horace Monash was an important athlete who would carry America's hopes down the Rhine River next year. His every look and demeanor gave him away. His clean-shaven, square-jawed face was absolutely symmetrical, a perfection further heightened by his hair, which was parted down the middle of his scalp and combed wavily straight back. He was slim-hipped, chesty, and big enough around the shoulders to make him a touch top-heavy. Just right for a swimmer, according to the observers on the seawall. His muscles were not knotty, either, or molded into concretelike blocks. This, too, was just right for a swimmer. Also, his legs were so powerful-looking they appeared able to outkick a five-horse engine. He moved gracefully and smoothly, walking always on the balls of his feet. He seemed to float or be walking on springs. Horace's body glistened with sweat and suntan lotion. The marvelous deep bronze color he had acquired was enhanced by the whiteness of his swimming suit. Horace Monash was a picture of physical grace and power. Each of his lady friends was awed and overwhelmed by his presence. They willingly served him. And if anyone had any doubts at all about Horace Monash the Olympic celebrity, the autographs he so graciously gave were the clincher.

"Well. What do you think, Rich?" I asked my brother who was dragging his fishing line with great sweeps of the pole in search of a fish. We were fishing out at the end of the jetty and watching Horace at the other end.

"Well? What do I think about what?"

"About Horace Monash."

"What about him?"

I felt a slight tug on my line, jerked the rod, and quickly reeled in. There was nothing on it. But the bait was gone. Something had a feast. Probably a crab. I slipped another fat sandworm onto a hook and cast the line out again. Neither Rich nor I had caught a fish in days.

"He never goes in the water any deeper than his knees. He never swims. Do you think he knows how?"

"How do I know?" Rich answered, sweeping his rod in a great arc and reeling in slowly. He was plainly irritated over his inability to hook a fluke. "I've never seen him swim. No one has. But that doesn't mean he can't. He sure looks like a swimmer to me. Long distance."

Ah! I thought. Another expert. "Hey. He's been down here every weekend since the Fourth. And come to think of it, he's been down here every day for the past week."

Horace was on vacation.

"He does setting-up exercises, deep knee bends, push-ups, and heaves that ten-ton medicine ball around with his girlfriend."

"Which one?" Rich wanted to know.

"What difference does it make. He still has not swum a stroke."

"Maybe he needs a few more days of conditioning before he does his stuff. You know as well as I do that a pitcher doesn't start throwing hard right away. He warms up to loosen up. And then he throws hard. Hey! I got one!"

Rich jerked the line, payed it out, choked the reel, and watched the line go taut. It stayed taut as Rich reeled it in. The fluke had no fight in it. The fish resisted being reeled in by trying to swim the other way. But when Rich reeled it out of the water, the fish just gave up. Rich unhooked it, threw it in a bushel basket where it flopped around for a few minutes and then lay still. He rebaited the hook and cast the line out again.

"You know what, Rich?" I persisted.

"What?"

"I don't think Horace Monash can swim."

"You've got to be kidding."

"Nope. You heard me right. I don't think he can swim!"

"You're talking through your hat. Sure he can swim. Everybody can swim. Mom swims. Dad swims. You swim. I swim. Everybody swims. Pretty soon Horace is going to jump into the water and swim all the way to Staten Island—a practice run—and back again."

"I'll tell you something, Rich. I happened to be up very early yesterday morning because I heard someone go rattling down the ladder. Everyone was still asleep, including you. The sun hadn't even risen high enough to burn off the haze. And there he was . . ."

"Who?"

"Horace! He was sneaking around on the beach all alone looking every which way as if to make sure no one was watching him. And do you know what he was doing?"

"No. What?"

"He was walking alongside the jetty—in the water—like he was looking for something. Only he wasn't looking for anything. The tide was coming in. He got smacked real good by a couple of breakers but he kept on walking. He had a long stick in his hand poking the depth of the water in front of him. He didn't go all the way out to the end. He knew enough not to be that stupid. But he did go out far enough to let the water reach his chest."

"Whew. And then what?"

"He stumbled all the way back, got a few more smacks of water and a mouthful that made him gag and cough like he was choking to death. He must have gotten banged up, too, because his legs were bleeding. Not badly. Just a scrape or two above his knees. Now. If he were a swimmer, he would have pushed himself away from the rocks and kind of let the tide and swells float him in. He's up to something, Rich. And he's going to drown himself doing it!"

"Don't look now. But here he comes."

I turned around and we both watched Horace crawl along the ridge of the rocks in our direction. He was sporting two Band-Aids on each leg.

"Hi, fellers," Horace cheerfully greeted us when he finally reached the end. "How're ya doing? Catch anything?"

"Fine," I replied. Rich held up the fluke.

"Great-looking fish. How much you want for it?"

"Nothing. It's not for sale."

"Why not? It's easy money. You'll catch another?"

"We're not selling because we're going to eat it tonight," Rich retorted.

"You fellers must know these waters around here."

"Yup."

"Do you have any idea how deep it is here—here at the end of the rocks?"

"Yup"

Rich shot a knowing "he's-going-to-do-it-I-told-you-so-he's-plotting-a-course-glance" at me.

"That depends on the tide," I told him. "When the tide is high and normal—no full moon . . ."

"Full moon?"

"Yeah. A full moon means very deep water at high tide and very

37

shallow water at low tide. When the tide is high and normal, no full moon," I repeated, "there's about nine or ten feet of water out here."

"What about low tide?"

"At low tide there's about four to six feet of water."

"That's not even over my head," Horace happily concluded.

"Don't let that fool you," I warned him.

"You're not planning a swim, are you?" Rich interrupted.

"You can count on it!"

"Do you want some advice, Mr. Monash?" I offered.

"No. Not really. Thank you just the same. You've told me all I need to know."

"Well, I'll give you some just the same. Swim on the bay side. Over there. On the right. High or low tide. It's always smooth as silk, calm and safe. No one ever got in any trouble over there so long as they didn't swim out too far."

"Trouble?"

"The sea side of the rocks—here, on the left—can be very dangerous. Sometimes it's too rough to swim here at high tide. Four- to five-foot breakers. You've seen them. Heavy debris coming into the rocks from the ocean. Very dangerous. Sometimes when its not so rough there's an undertow that can drag on a good swimmer and make it tough to get out of the water. Maybe you haven't noticed but there's a very strong current at low tide. It begins just off the end of the rocks and goes out to sea for about ten or fifteen miles."

"Len's right, Mr. Monash," Rich declared. "The current is something! Even good swimmers can get in trouble. If they don't panic they can get out of it by floating with it or swimming under-water at an angle. If you panic or can't swim at all, forget it. You're dead! No one will go in there to get you."

"And they'll find your body ten minutes later floating off Crooke's Point, Staten Island, four miles from here," I added for emphasis. "If they don't find your body off Crooke's Point, then it's fifteen miles out to sea and the sharks will have had you for dinner. Gone. Goodbye."

"Even though it's not over anyone's head except a midget's?" Horace asked in disbelief.

"Yup. It takes six minutes to die in the current and ten minutes to find your body off Crooke's Point. Two people died because they were swept past the tidal pole and had nothing to hang on to. Another died of exhaustion fighting the current."

I had no idea if my arithmetic or even my tale about drownings was accurate. A slight exaggeration was not far from the truth, anyway. The current was fast and deadly. People did drown in it. I do not know how many. Two strong men on two oars in a rowboat could not make headway against the current. No matter how hard they rowed they would lose ground. Small boats full of amateur fishermen and summer people would often fall victim to the current. Motorized cruisers or small boats rigged with outboard engines would tow them into the bay for a price. It wasn't unusual to see one Owens or Wheeler cruiser towing a string of twelve or fifteen rowboats past the current's power and danger.

"You fellers are kidding me, aren't you? You're trying to scare me. I like that. You've got imagination. But I don't scare easily! How do you like that?"

"We don't kid about things like that, Mr. Monash. We've seen it happen a few times. So suit yourself."

"I guess he knows what he's doing," Rich remarked as we watched Horace clumsily work his way back to the beach and his girlfriend of the day.

"Look at that, Rich! He's no athlete on the rocks. Whoops! Look out! He's going to slip into the water!" No such luck. Horace grabbed a rock and held on.

Rich and I went back to our fishing. A couple of nasty flies were biting our sunburned backs. The current was coming alive as the tide continued to ebb. The saving of Mrs. Franks, a young mother with two small children, jumped into my mind. It wasn't so long ago. Only last summer. It was a Saturday when the beach and water on the sea side of the rocks was unusually crowded.

Elsie Franks was a strong swimmer. She decided to swim on the bay side of the jetty to avoid the crowd. She dived in, leaving her two children with her husband. She swam straight out past the jetty's point. When she reached a spot a couple of hundred yards from the beach—she was way out—she turned and headed in with a slow, steady stroke. But the tide was going out and carrying her to the water on the other side of the jetty. She swam straight into the current. Before Elsie Franks knew what had happened, she was suddenly swept into the tide pole where luckily she was able to hang on to a thick clump of seaweed. A small cruiser picked her up and returned her to the beach. It had taken Elsie Franks a leisurely half hour to swim two hundred yards out into the bay and less than five minutes to be swept five hundred yards into the tide pole!

Now it was another summer, the Sunday of Labor Day weekend, September 1, to be exact. This was the day Horace decided to take the plunge.

It was a warm, soggy, and overcast morning. The tide was well out. The water was flat and glassy. A half-dozen rowboats were anchored off the jetty beyond the far side of the current. Their sleepy occupants were fishing. A seventh rowboat was tethered to the tide pole with a line long enough to keep it out of the current. It didn't matter much anyway since the rowboat was equipped with a one-and-a-half horsepower outboard engine.

Horace and his girlfriend for the Labor Day weekend were alone on the beach, sitting in the wet sand at the water's edge letting the water lap over their legs. I was out on the end of the jetty trying to free some snarled fishing lines trapped in the seaweed on the underside of the rocks. Rich was sitting on the seawall watching the fishermen in rowboats through a pair of binoculars trying to see what fish they were catching if any.

Horace stood and donned a white rubber bathing cap that covered his ears. Rich trained his binoculars on Horace. Horace stretched a pair of goggles over his eyes and walked into the water—not far—just about ten feet from the current's beachside edge. There, he flopped on his belly in a "dead man's float" in about three and a half feet of water. At least it looked like a dead man's float to his girlfriend who exhorted him on to more activity jumping up and down and clapping her hands. To Rich, sitting above them on the seawall, Horace was not floating at all. His head was facedown in the water. His arms were stretched out ahead of him. But only one leg was stiff in the water behind him. The other leg was below the surface groping for the sandy bottom.

Rich watched Horace find some footing and push himself a little. Still pushing, Horace managed to turn himself around, face the beach, and breast-stroke his way back a few feet. Wet and sandy, Horace fell out of the water, picked himself up, leaped up onto the jetty, and began to work his way to the end. His girlfriend was right behind him.

I saw them coming. "Go to it, Money Honey," the girl urged Horace. "Swim, champ. Show me how it's done."

Now I knew what he was up to, finally. So did Rich, who was

now scrambling toward us on the rocks yelling, "Don't do it! Don't do it!"

"Don't do it, Mr. Monash," I repeated. "Don't do it. You'll drown. There's no lifeguard out here."

"What! Me drown in that bathtub out there? Don't be silly. Look how calm it is. It's low tide and it does not even come up to my neck. You told me so yourself, remember?"

"It's not so calm, Mr. Monash. Do you see the current over there?"

Horace waved me off. "And may I remind you, young feller, that I do not scare so easily."

"You tell this kid, Money Honey. Show the boy what kind of stuff a real he-man is made of."

"You don't know how to swim, Mr. Monash," Rich coolly added. "I've been watching you. You can't swim," he persisted.

"What? Are you crazy? Me not know how to swim? Stick around, kid. Maybe you'll learn a trick or two in the water."

"I bet," Rich responded with contempt.

Horace ignored us. He winked at his lady friend, adjusted his cap, and pulled the goggles over his eyes. For an instant he struck an erect and muscular pose of affirmation and confidence. He flexed his biceps for good measure. Horace Monash was finally possessed by his own immortality, borne on the winds of a lady's urgings, and his own assessment of his strength pitted against shallow water. He would handle the sea as he handled the dead weight of the medicine ball—with conspicuous ease. No problem. This was his time.

"Don't, Mr. Monash!" Rich and I cried out together.

But he did! God knows why. He knew he couldn't swim. It would have been just as easy to walk into the water from the beach. But no! Horace had to take a flying leap. He leaped out and away from the rocks into six feet of water. It was deeper then he had figured on. His long legs could not find the bottom. A slight swell caught him over his head and nudged him back toward the rocks. It was as if the sea itself was sending Horace a message: "This is no place for you. Go back to the rocks, to the beach, where you belong."

Horace's nose and mouth filled with the briny water. A string of seaweed wrapped itself around his neck and began to strangle him. He swallowed hard and gagged. Horace tore the seaweed off his neck as he groped wildly for the rocks and solid footing. He found neither. As another wave came off the rocks it picked him up like a floating cork. It carried him into the current beyond. There his legs were yanked out from under him. And there, in that split second, as he was being dragged feetfirst and on his back through the deceptive current, Horace Monash began a race with time for his life.

"Don't fight it, Mr. Monash!" I screamed at the top of my lungs. "Float! Float with it!"

"He can't swim," Rich kept muttering.

Horace was beyond sound. He couldn't hear a thing. His bathing cap and goggles had been ripped from his head partly from the speed of the water and partly from his own wild thrashing. If Horace heard anything at all it was the sound of water running by and into his ears.

Then Rich hopped and skipped back along the jetty yelling, "Man in the water! Man in the water! Help! Help!"

Horace's girlfriend was frozen with horror. She stared wide-eyed and speechless in a partial rigid crouch at the fast disappearing Horace. The sluggish fishermen in the rowboats woke up. People appeared at the seawall. Horace was now three-quarters of the way toward the tide pole taking on water, beginning to fight less and to sink more.

The two men in the outboard-rigged rowboat tethered to the tide pole caught a glimpse of Horace in the current and in trouble. One of them quickly started up the engine and slowly edged toward the pole. Horace came at them like a torpedo. They maneuvered the boat between the oncoming Horace and the tide pole while still tied to the pole. Partially submerged and nearly unconscious, Horace slammed into the rowboat. He was immediately grabbed, plucked out of the water, and hauled into the boat. The boat was unhitched and made for the beach where a small crowd had gathered to watch the drama. The boat was driven up onto the sand. Several willing hands reached in and pulled the limp Horace Monash from the boat.

"Easy does it. He's still got some life in him."

Horace, half awake and helpless, was stretched facedown, his head and the rest of him sloping toward the water. One of his rescuers was straddling him and administering artificial respiration. A Sea Gate police car, responding to a call, arrived on the scene. A sweating cop whose leathery face reflected numerous death-dealing encounters in his professional life, clamped a respirator on Horace's face.

"This is a fairly new gadget," he shouted into Horace's ear. "Sometimes it works. Sometimes it doesn't. Cross your fingers. Can you hear me?"

Horace moaned. He twitched a little, retched, and came back to life. Sympathetic onlookers helped him to his wobbly feet. Horace, swaying unsteadily, looked around for his girlfriend. She had recovered from her momentary trauma and was spotted fleeing toward the seawall ladder.

"Some Olympic swimmer!" she cried out from the ladder. "What a line!" she yelled, pushing her way past a young doctor who had arrived with an ambulance from Coney Island Hospital. "Cream puff!" she continued. "Bread crumb!"

Horace stumbled over to the flat rock where he had spent so much of the summer spinning his lying web of Olympic glory to catch a gullible female. The trouble was he was so convincing he caught himself in his own trap and believed his own lies. Now it was all gone—girls and glory—shattered at the jetty by a willful sea. Horace lay down with his face to the sun that had now burned through the gray day. The doctor looked at Horace, listened to his heart, sat him up, thumped him a bit, stood him up, and walked him around.

"You're in better shape than I'm in. You don't need a hospital. From what I've heard you need a psychiatrist and a cup of coffee. Go home. Rest. Stay out of the water for a day or two."

"A day or two!" exclaimed the cop. He had finished writing his report. All that was left to do was obtain Horace's name, address, and telephone number. "This guy shouldn't even take a bath. He may not be safe in the shower, either!"

"What a shame," sighed a tall elegant lady from the Sans Souci Lodge, a summer hotel. "And such a handsome specimen. America has lost a great Olympic swimmer."

"What great Olympic swimmer?" demanded a bearded bystander. "I know him from the city. He's Horace Monash, the salad maker at Lindy's on Times Square."

The policeman drove Horace back to his rented room having first provided him with a steaming mug of coffee from a thermos.

"Stay home, buddy. Be good to yourself. Stay out of the ocean. I don't make salads. I don't even try."

Horace Monash, silent and back to reality, packed up his belongings and left the next morning—Labor Day—on the *Mayflower*'s early 9 A.M. holiday run to the Battery. Rich and I watched the boat emerge from Gravesend Bay as we prepared our fishing gear for a day on the jetty. I waved. No one waved back. But the captain responded with one long and three short blasts of the whistle:

"Departing. Hail and Farewell."

1936 _____

For most of the winter of 1935–1936, the winds howled and drove the heaving sea into the jetty without relief. When the tide was low cold blasts of arctic air froze the briny spray to the rocks in an ever-thickening mass of ice.

At high tide, the incoming Atlantic rolled over the ice-coated jetty and slammed obliquely into the seawall with a continuous roar as it merged with Gravesend Bay. The air was damp and clammy. Everything everywhere was sticky with the humid sea. For days on end, week after wet week, the sun, hidden behind a constant veil of low scudding clouds and salty sprays, shed a sickly light on the Lower Bay. It snowed heavily a few times but none of it stuck to the shoreline—only inland. It would take the coming spring to begin the dry-out. And it would take all spring for a newly emerged sun to finally spread its warming heat over a sea spent from its winter struggle—exhausted from its fruitless violence against the jetty—from hurling its mighty power at the rocks in vain.

The ice melted. The ocean rested. The jetty stood. It was summer once more.

I went back out on the rocks again to survey my world. It was a somewhat altered world than the one I had known last summer. King George V of England had died during the winter. England had a new king, Edward VIII. I felt badly about that. I did not know King George V or anything about him except what I read and saw on the shiny pages of the *National Geographic* magazine. I had felt a strange emptiness when Calvin Coolidge died three years ago. He was president when I was born. I was overcome with the same strangeness three years before that when Chief Justice and ex-President William Howard Taft and his own grandfather died during the same month. And somewhere, deep down, I hoped that Franklin Delano Roosevelt would be reelected president of the United States in November just so that things would remain as is—familiar—safe—forever.

But the world would not stay quiet for me, not even there on the end of the rocks. I watched a parade of the world's greatest ocean liners leave New York for their home ports in England, France, Sweden, Germany, and Italy.

There were one or two American ships. These beauties were all jammed with business travelers and pleasure seekers. And I sat there, on the rocks, looking and wondering about the daily headlines:

MUSSOLINI TAKES ETHIOPIA!

HAILE SELASSIE FLEES ON BRITISH WARSHIP!

REBELLION IN SPAIN!

GERMANY ANNEXES THE RHINELAND!

That brooding, menacing, screaming man with a mustache, Adolf Hitler, did what he said he would do: let a German army loose in Europe again. Bah! What am I getting myself all worked up over? It's all so far away. And far away, too, are the Japanese making war on China. That's been going on for four years. Too far away for me to bother about. Let the old folks talk about "the world going mad." I've got my rocks, the ships leaving with the outgoing tide, and fish waiting to be caught. Peace!

"Hey, kid!"

The gravelly voice belonged to a thin, hawkish man under a straw hat. He was sitting behind and above me on a particularly jagged boulder.

"Oh. Hi, T. D."

T. D. was new to the jetty and the neighborhood. "T. D." had nothing to do with his name. Only his landlady knew his name. She never mentioned it to anyone. T. D. himself took great pains to avoid proper introductions and only gave a number T7461389D. The "T" and "D" were part of the number. He claimed the initials stood for "the damned." When I first heard them I thought they stood for "touchdown," figuring that T. D. must have been his nickname when he was a football player. And I didn't know that he was ever a football player. I was only guessing. It was a terrible guess at that. T. D. was too skinny, small, and wiry to have ever been a football player. He looked like he could squeeze himself through the straw of a milk shake.

After a while T. D. let some of his secret out if not his name. And he made no bones about it. He had been a convict. His home for fourteen years had been Alcatraz in San Francisco Bay where, he complained, "they took away his name." "Connections" brought him east to work in the bootlegging racket after his release. But when he arrived in Brooklyn, the Prohibition Act was repealed making smuggling booze unnecessary. T. D. found himself "disconnected" and jobless.

He found work soon enough punching holes in the ride tickets inside George C. Tilyou's gigantic Steeplechase Amusement Park in nearby Coney Island. Later he was promoted. He became a seller of admission tickets to the park. Everyone who came to Coney Island for fun, frozen custard, cotton candy, and Nathan's hot dogs, saw and heard T. D. sell tickets. For T. D., all these people could remain nameless like himself. Boys and girls were all "Kid." A grown man was always "Mac." Women were all "Sister."

During the spring, T. D. moved into a small apartment facing a treeless, weedy acre at the edge of the seawall called "Lindberg Park." He lived alone. But he was not without friends. There was Amiel the Gardener who earned a meager living cutting grass and hedges. Nobody knew his last name. It could be that Amiel himself could not remember his last name. He was stewed, crocked, besotted, inebriated, soaked, crapulous, intoxicated—plain drunk!—much of the time. Amiel was an ancient, bowlegged gentleman in overalls who claimed that if it were not for his illegitimate birth, he would be a Belgian prince, if not the king himself. No one really knew what Amiel looked like, either. He sported a huge droopy, gray handlebar mustache that covered his entire face below his nose. He wore a wide-brimmed straw hat, too, that completely shaded his face and which he removed only when sleep overcame him. At that moment, he would remove his hat and cover his face with it.

T. D. had another couple of pals—two brothers—George and Gavin Garwood. They were left stranded and penniless by a millionaire father who went broke during the Great Depression and never recovered. He eventually met his end in a wild leap off the Brooklyn Bridge. His body was never found. George, the elder, cut grass and hedges, too, to stay alive—there were plenty to go around—while Gavin watched him. George also was able to do small plumbing and woodwork repair that improved his income from time to time. Gavin always went along with George on these jobs to watch and to give advice.

Once in a while Amiel, George, Gavin, and T. D. would get

50

together in T. D.'s apartment and have themselves a very quiet, boozy party that would last through the night into the early morning hours.

T. D. could see the tip of the jetty from his living room window. His view of the bay was partially blocked by a two-story house with a sinister name—the "Bootlegger's House." Needless to say, when the boys were having one of their parties, the view from the living room window hardly mattered.

Very often, at low tide, T. D. would come to the jetty's end and sit cross-legged on the jagged boulder. This was one of those times.

"Watcha know, kid?"

"What do I know about what?"

"About anything. Like those ships out there. Watcha know about them? Some parade, eh, kid?"

"Well, the first three-stacker that went by—the one leading the parade—is the *Queen Mary*. She's English. The biggest and fastest in the world. She won the Blue Ribbon a couple of months ago. Beat the German right behind her—the *Bremen*. It took her only four days to go from Southampton to Ambrose Light. The next one, the one after the *Bremen*, is French. She's the *Normandie*— the very modern-looking one with three stacks."

"Who's next?"

"The *Rex*. Italian. She's very fast, too. Then there's the *Gripsholm*, the one with the two tan stacks and blue stack insignias. Swedish. The three-stacker coming through the narrows now is the *Leviathan*. American. She used to be German."

"No kidding?"

"Yup. German. The *vaterland*. We captured her at her pier on the Hudson during the World War."

"Now. How did you know that? I was in the war, you know.

Over in France. Got captured. Spent five months a prisoner of war. Prisons are my whole life."

"I didn't know that. My dad told me."

"Did he capture the ship?"

"Nope. He worked on her—changing her from the world's largest passenger ship—at that time, anyway—to the world's largest troopship and back again."

"Some sight. All them boats, eh, kid? And all them people going where the boats will take them. Anywhere. Everywhere."

"Ships, T. D. Ships."

"Yeah. Ships. Never saw anything like it from the Rock."

"You mean Alcatraz?"

"Yeah. Alcatraz. Nope. They had big ships out there on the coast, too, you know. The *President* this and the *President* that. I remember a big bugger. The *Matsonia*. We could hear their band playing Hawaiian music everytime she left and "California, Here I Come" every time she'd arrive. But nothing like these babies, though. These are monsters. Mostly there were a lot of small fishing boats and sailboats tearing around 'Frisco Bay; freighters, tankers, tramps, and such. I would have taken any one of them if I had half a chance."

"You mean escape," I gasped.

"Are you kidding? Sure. Escape! And what would have been so terrible. A nice sea voyage to Singapore or Shanghai would have set me up real good. Let me tell you, me and the boys thought up plenty of schemes to 'fly.' But by the time we'd figure out a good one and worked out every last detail, fourteen years had gone by and I was out legally. No one gets off the Rock just like that, kid," T. D. said with a snap of his fingers.

"I read somewhere that a few cons—er—excuse me, T. D., I meant to say inmates . . ."

52

"That's okay, kid. I like con better. Everybody knows what a con is. Can you imagine calling movie tough guys like Jimmy Cagney and Edward G. Robinson inmates?"

"Okay, T. D. You win. But I read about a couple of escapes from Alcatraz."

"Yeah. Sure. In dime novels. Or maybe in the movies. I'm telling you, kid, the Rock was maximum security, federal. One time I was working the rock pile because I refused to eat the garbage we were handed for breakfast and dinner. We didn't have lunch. I used to work the rock pile a lot; good, steady, outside work. The rocks out there were a lot like these. I thought up a solid idea for flying. I didn't tell a soul. All I did was think about it. And along comes this bull."

"Bull?"

"Yeah. Bull! Guard! Cop! Bull! You get my meaning? Bull! And he says to me, 'You thinking of flying?' And he didn't mean in an airplane. 'Just thinking,' I told him. And just for thinking of about how nice it would be on the outside I got three days in the hole—in solitary."

"Wow! That's awful!"

"Naw. Not so bad as it sounds. I didn't have to be anywhere special. The three days I was out of circulation didn't matter. I had a few years to go on the inside. It was like a three-day vacation. Anything was better than chopping rocks. I got fed regularly in my not-so-fancy private dining room. I had a window—very small, mind you, but a window with a view. I could see the boats and San Francisco. I got a rest.

"After I did ten they offered me a parole. I wouldn't go. They said I had to go. So I hit a bull—clobbered him pretty good with a shovel. Then they said I couldn't go and gave me five for hitting the bull. Five years later, the warden asked me, 'Who are you going to belt today?" 'No one' I said. 'Why?' And he says, 'You're out as of noon tomorrow.' I didn't hit anyone. I took in the free air. And sometimes I wonder why."

"How can you say a thing like that, T. D.? Isn't it much better to be free and sitting on these rocks than chopping away a prison rock pile?"

His answer startled me.

"Free? It's all in the way you look at it, kid. I have no family. You can count my friends on the fingers of one hand—Amiel—the Garwoods—maybe you, if that's okay with you?"

"Sure."

"Here on the outside—it's been three years now—I have to take care of myself. There's no one to look after me. No one knows if I'm sick or dying. But on the inside. Now. That's different. They feed me, give me clothes, fix my teeth, put me in a hospital if I'm really bad off, give me a bed, soap, towel, toothbrush and toothpaste. What's more, they pay me a couple of bucks a month for the work I do so's I can buy cigarettes, and maybe even a candy bar. I don't have to think hard about everything on the outside. I don't have to decide on anything. If I had been smart when I was younger I would have stayed in the army. The army would have taken care of me just like the prison except they'd let me out regularly so's I could enjoy myself once in a while."

"Jeez, T. D. You sound like you miss the place."

"Maybe. I just think the world out here is too complicated and more dangerous than on the inside. On the inside, everyone knows his place—what a con can or cannot do. If a con steps out of line with other cons—zap! His lights go out for good. He's taken care of. If a con steps out of line with the bulls—zap! He'll learn never to cross a bull again. So he tries not to step out of line. Sometimes it can't be helped, stepping out of line, like the time I did. Every con gets into trouble once in his life on the inside. You need a little action, a little excitement. You know, variety in your life.

"But here on the outside, people are nuts. They want too many things—more than they'll ever need or use. Take that clown Hitler. He keeps screaming that Germany needs this and needs that. Maybe so. But what he says Germany needs belongs to someone else. Only he says it doesn't. Just like a Chicago hood. So what does he do? He makes it look legit by putting everyone in a snappy uniform, hands them a rod, and tells them to go grab what's theirs but isn't. Just like a hood. Don't worry about a thing he tells everyone, the army will do the taking, as if that makes it legit.

"They're doing a lot of marching around over there and the people like it. They don't have to take care of themselves anymore. They don't even have to think. Germany—Hitler—will take care of them and do the thinking. Hell, I used to belong to gangs like that. We had plenty of rods. No uniforms, though. The boss did the thinking and we did the heisting. Life was uncomplicated. They called us criminals and gangsters. So—what else is new? We all got ten to fifteen on the Rock, in Leavenworth, Sing Sing, and other select palaces like that. Hitler would be doing fifteen to twenty by now if he played by the same rules we did—and he sure as hell does! Maybe they can get him on an income tax rap like Al Capone. When all else fails the feds, they get you on taxes! Maybe they don't have income taxes in *Deutschland Uber Alles.*"

"But isn't that what you say you like, T. D.? An uncomplicated life—the kind you had on the inside? And aren't the Germans doing what you said you would have done had you been smarter—join the army?"

"That's just it, kid. There's a big difference between being unarmed and being taken care of on the inside, and being armed on the outside to grab what isn't yours. You don't hear Roosevelt screaming his head off about wanting Mexico. Or Canada. And then sending troops into those places telling the people they had always been a part of the Great U S of A, do you? My kind of army wasn't interested in complications. Them Germans start out simple like having a friendly beer and then complicate everything."

T. D. was confusing me and I told him so.

"That's what I mean. It's all so complicated, it's dangerous. Take all those boats—er—ships out there—English, German, Italian, French, Swedish, American—you name it."

"Here comes a Japanese freighter," I pointed out.

"How do you know she's Japanese?" T. D. wanted to know, momentarily interrupting his world commentary.

"She's got three white stripes running around the tops of her black funnels. She's riding very low in the water. She's so heavy with something she looks partially awash and submerged, almost like she was sneaking out, while looking over her shoulder to be sure she was not being followed. Only Japanese freighters leave New York looking like that. And they always seem to move faster than other ships, like they were in a big hurry."

"Yeah. Okay, kid. Add the Japanese to the list. Now. You think these ships are parading. Right? No! Look again."

I shielded my eyes from the bright sun with my hands and squinted hard. I had pretty good eyes. I could read the names of the ships right off their bows and transoms a mile or two miles away—depending on the size of the letters.

"Looks like a parade to me."

"They are sneaking after each other," T. D. went on. "They're

56

tracking each other; sniffing each other like a pack of dogs; getting ready to outmaneuver the other guy on the open sea. They're so jealous of each other they'll all end up on the bottom someday for no good reason.

"Everything looks nice and peaceful out there now." T. D. wouldn't let up. "Flags. Color. Bands. Orchestras. Booze. Parties. Good times. All them people have everything they need right now. But in a couple of years—maybe three, maybe four—when they run out of things to do and want more than what they've got, and someone says you can't have any more than what you already got, all them people are going to get a little meaner each day until they run amuck. Then they'll blow themselves and each other right out of the water they think belongs to them."

I wasn't sure I understood all that T. D. was trying to get across.

"You will," he assured me as he lifted himself off the rock and stretched. "It's going to be a lot safer on the inside than the outside when the shooting starts. I don't know what I'm doing on the outside. It's tough and it's going to get tougher."

"You're not thinking of going back on the inside, are you, T. D.?"

"No, I guess not. I just do a lot of talking. Too much maybe. I really like it here. It's got the same salty, fishy smell as the Rock. I feel like I belong a little bit. When I look out of my window at the bay and these rocks I feel like I'm back on familiar territory. I'm at home on these rocks. I can see everything clearly. I can think. And I can think straight. I suppose I'll stay that way. Straight. See you around, kid."

"See you around, T. D.," I called after him as T7461389D scrambled off the jetty.

1937

"Well? What do you think of it, Len?" Marcella Marchand wanted to know. She was holding up a watercolor for me to inspect. The painting was partly covered by a shadow from the huge, wide-brimmed straw hat she was wearing. "I've never painted a seascape before, you know. Only landscapes."

"It looks okay to me, except . . ." That's as far as I dared go momentarily. I wasn't sure I had a license to be critical.

Marcella Marchand was old enough to be my mother. In fact, she was the mother of a friend of mine, Mac Marchand. But more than that, Marcella Marchand was a professional painter who exhibited regularly at the Macbeth Gallery in Manhattan. I was not altogether sure that the question required an answer or that an answer was being sought. Nonetheless, given my momentary hesitation, and my itch to say something, I became a critic.

"The water is too blue. That water out there is gray today and every day. It just isn't as blue as you painted it. And there are three boats out there, not one. And . . ."

"You are absolutely right, young man. That water is gray. And there are three boats. I went to school, too, you know. I can count. And I do know the difference between blue and gray."

"Then how come your painting is so different?"

"First of all, I could say that two people looking at the very same thing could see it two different ways. Some of us are nearsighted. Some of us are farsighted. Some are color-blind. Many of us know very little about what we are looking at. We may see but not know. And few of us know a great deal about what we see. All of these differences, and lots more, cause two different people to see an object or a scene differently. Wouldn't you say?"

"I suppose so."

"Good. But I do not want to say those things. Frankly, I am not interested in copying what you think or even what I think I see. I am more interested in changing what we both think we see—however differently we see it—into something that I believe would be an improvement over what is actually there. Does that make sense to you?"

"No."

"Let's just say that I painted those things out there—the water, boat, sky—as I should like them to be, not as they are or seem to be. How does that sound? Better?"

"No. The painting still does not look like what it's supposed to look like!" Marcella sighed and shook her head. She and I had been debating in a circle of sun. It was the only patch of brightness on a cloudy August afternoon. Somehow, the sun had found a crack in the overcast sky and sent a beam of light to the jetty. For a while the sunbeam was so fixed and unmoving that the best of stage designers could not have devised a more dramatic or theatrical illusion.

But now, the show was over. The sun was gone. A gray day in the middle of August, when days were usually clear, dry, and crisp, was always a harbinger of the coming autumn. The season was waning. School was three weeks off. The summer was playing itself out.

59

Marcella began another painting but quickly decided against it. She tore the heavy paper from the pad, crumpled it, and tossed it like a ball into the water.

"I'm not sure that seascapes are my strength," she moaned as she surveyed the rocks for possible subjects. Marcella flipped up her wide-brimmed straw hat and squinted hard at the rocks.

"These rocks have structural mass to them," Marcella observed. "They communicate such contained power and reliability that I get the feeling that if the earth suddenly blew up, all that would be left would be these rocks—this jetty—maybe along with Michelangelo's *Moses* or his *David*."

I half heard Marcella as she rustled her papers and prepared to go to work on a painting of the rocks.

A tugboat appeared from around the bend on the ocean side. Marcella paid it no mind. She had leaned into the watercolor with deliberate strokes, humming some unidentifiable tune while working her way across the paper. The tug, heading for the Narrows, was pulling five empty barges against the tide without a struggle.

As if without warning, the tug and its barges focused my attention on Hoffman Island in the background and T. D. jumped into my head. Hoffman Island triggered an image of Alcatraz three thousand miles away. I had heard that T7461389D was back in prison—maybe not Alcatraz—Leavenworth, Kansas, more likely. He probably had a different number, too.

T. D. had not stayed "straight" after all. He was caught at something petty and stupid—shortchanging customers at Steeplechase Amusement Park in neighboring Coney Island. If the admission ticket to the park was a dollar and a half and the customer handed over a five-dollar bill, T. D. returned three dollars in counterfeit bills folded in half as if the fifty cents coming was included. It wasn't. T. D. pocketed the legitimate three fifty. He tried it once too often. His last victim was a United States Treasury agent. T. D. was immediately arrested, handcuffed, and taken to the Eighth Street Precinct where he was temporarily incarcerated before being dragged to a federal court for passing counterfeit bills in acts of grand larceny.

The more I thought about it the more I was convinced that T. D. had planned his crime just to go back to the "inside." The last I saw of him, maybe six months ago, T. D. had become distant and morose, convinced that most of the population was too dangerous to the rest to be allowed to run around free—including himself.

"We're all nuts out here," he had cautioned me. "Some of us are harmless. Some of us are not. And it's getting worse. Too complicated. It's safer inside."

T. D. could have been right. Since January, the world beyond the jetty had become more restless. England had still another king. The old one, uncrowned Edward VIII, wanted to marry Wally Simpson, an American woman. The whole idea gave such fits to the English that Edward quit—abdicated—"for the woman I love." His brother became King George VI.

There's more.

Adolf Hitler screamed over our Stromberg-Carlson radio as if he were in the same room with us. And the whole of Germany roared behind him. *"Zeig Heil! Zeig Heil! Zeig Heil!"* They always did it three times. The world owed him something was about the gist of it. And the German nation agreed. It sounded like they were going to get it!

Benito Mussolini stood on balconies all over Italy and screamed something. He didn't want to be left out. He strutted around,

jut-jawed with arms akimbo listening to the crowd roar apprecia-
tively, *"Il Duce! Il Duce! Il Duce!"* Whatever it was he wanted,
the great crowds in the piazzas of Rome and elsewhere were going
to get it for him!

A half a world away, Japanese planes bombed Tientsin, China.
They captured Peking and shelled Nankow. The newspapers were
full of the madness. And the Japanese gave their cheer three times,
too! "Banzai! Banzai! Banzai!"

So what! All that was so far away it didn't matter. But the
distance between them and us would suddenly grow shorter at the
end of the year when Japanese planes would attack an American
gunboat, the USS *Panay,* in the Yangtze River, and kill Americans.

Spain had become a bloody battleground. There, a civil war
raged on in which several Italian divisions and German warplanes
assisted the Nationalist forces. It was not their fight. But they were
there, anyway. It was good, realistic training!

In Louisville, Kentucky, on the first Saturday in May, a brilliant
horse won the Derby. He went on to earn the Triple Crown by
winning the Preakness and Belmont races. The horse was called
War Admiral, a name with an ominous ring.

A few days later, late Thursday afternoon, May 6, I looked up
from my perch at the end of the jetty and watched the mammoth
German airship, *Hindenberg,* glide by at an astonishing low
altitude. It had begun to rain lightly, more of a mist than a rain.
The 803-foot-long airship, the largest machine in the sky, seemed
to go on endlessly. I could see people in the forward gondola
clearly. One of them waved. The dirigible, full of flammable,
lighter-than-air hydrogen, was heading across Lower Bay toward
Lakehurst, New Jersey, forty-five miles southwest of where I sat.
She was completing her thirty-sixth transatlantic crossing—

Germany to America. Two hours after I watched the *Hindenburg* disappear into the mist above the bay she reached Lakehurst and blew up!

The explosion was awesome, a portent of things to come.

If I had sensed a new reality, there seemed to be no urgency in it. I was separated from imminent danger by the hypnotic swells of the gently rolling sea and the vast, unthreatening view from the jetty. And however disquieting events had or would become, the euphoric pleasantness of Lower New York Bay as seen from the end of the jetty in August 1937, gave no hint of the nastiness in the rest of the world. I was a boy at peace on the Lower Bay as I watched the tug and its barges surge against the currents and become a blur in the Narrows.

I thought dreamily of the upcoming World Series. It would be the Yankees and the Giants. No contest. The Yankees all the way! In a couple of weeks, England's Tommy Farr would step into a boxing ring with Joe Louis, America's newly crowned heavyweight champion of the world. England makes good ships. But whoever heard of an English fighter. I gave Farr two or three rounds before being decked by Louis. But Tommy Farr would show the world what England was made of. He would go the distance—fifteen rounds—with the Brown Bomber and finish on his feet, bloodied, but on his feet. Tommy Farr, Englishman, would not go down for anyone.

"How do you like this?" Marcella asked, thrusting a watercolor at me, and waking me from my dreamy thoughts.

"It looks like the rocks."

"Marvelous! But is that all you have to say?"

"Well. They are not the rocks, exactly."

"You mean they are but they aren't."

"In a way. I can tell they are the rocks because they are deep green and rusty and jagged and all that. Water doesn't look like that. Boats don't look like that. So they have to be the rocks."

"But?"

"But nothing!"

"You mean they do not look like an exact duplication, like what a camera might take. Is that it?"

"That's right. You left out the detail, the bits and pieces of muscovite and biotite in the granite—the strings of dried seaweed—the clumps of wet seaweed—and mussels. Your rocks are too smooth. These rocks are full of nooks and crannies. They are grainy and not as brightly colored as you made them."

"Oh! Len," Marcella sighed. "Someday you will find out the difference between what the camera sees and what we humans would like to see. The difference between impression and expression—art and life. If I wanted to paint a picture of these rocks for no other reason than to paint these rocks, to show people what they look like, then I should do it as you say. I should give them their proper appearance as I believe it to be. But I am not interested in painting a memory of these rocks at a particular time of day."

"If you are not interested in painting the rocks then why do you paint them?" A logical question.

"Before I answer that, first tell me, do you like this little painting just as a little painting? Forget, for a moment whether or not the rocks are painted to appear as you say they should appear. What I am asking is, if you never saw this jetty in your whole life, would this picture interest you?"

"Yes, I think it would."

"Aaaaaaaaaaaaah! Good boy! You have possibilities. Now. Do you mind telling me why?"

"I really don't know why, except that I like the colors. And I like the way your rocks seem to fit together with their shadows and everything."

"Splendid!"

"I don't know what else to say except that the picture makes me think about things but I don't know what things. It's strange."

"That's good, indeed, my young friend. Now I'll tell you why I paint the rocks even though, as you say, I am not interested in them. I see the rocks as a symbol—a symbol of power—power to hold back the sea, the storm, and every thunderbolt."

I looked down the length of the jetty as Marcella raved on about the strength of the rocks. They were a tough, unyielding collection of stone blocks, all right. It didn't take much to figure that out. They had been breaking up the tides for years—since 1907, in fact—a little tidbit I had picked up from that old geologist who lectured me a couple of years back.

"These rocks are eternal," Marcella continued while the light in her green eyes brightened like sparklers on the Fourth of July. "Look at them, Len. Ancient. Massive. Silent. Structural. They are forever!"

I looked again. One of the boulders by itself might not have made such an impression. But a hundred of them locked together in a rambling arrangement was different, all right.

"There is an order, an arrangement to everything in the universe," Marcella observed. "Everything. Animal. Vegetable. Mineral. The rocks fall in the mineral category. There is a pattern and rhythm to it all. And artists try to understand these things so that we can rearrange the order—improve on it. I can see the struggle in the rocks."

"Struggle?"

Marcella ignored my query. "There in the shadows," she continued, "and recesses, in the highlights and halftones are the signs of eternal struggle, one rock set against another, all of them thrown together in a haphazard arrangement for a reason—for a purpose. There is motion here but nothing moves. There is combat here but nothing fights. All this granite, this jumble of—"

"Schist," I interrupted her impassioned observations. "None of this is granite. It's schist. Manhattan schist. And it's a million years old."

"Well, whatever. Schist, you say. Okay! A million years old, you say. Okay! Marvelous. Another good reason why this jumble of rocks is a symbol of immortality. They were there at the beginning and for them there is no end. I must get on with the painting of these rocks."

"I still don't get the symbol idea," I told her.

"Look at it this way, Len. To some people the painting of an apple on a tablecloth is just that: an apple on a tablecloth. To other people the painting of an apple being bitten in the Garden of Eden by a naked lady called Eve is more than just an apple. It is now called 'forbidden fruit,' a symbol of the first sin. But you would not know about such things, would you?"

Naked ladies? What is she talking about? Of course I knew about naked ladies. I'd seen them in paintings at the Metropolitan Museum. I'd seen one or two on the beach from a distance of about three hundred yards. A little closer in some magazines. But what they had to do with the rocks escaped me. Besides, I was more interested at the line of ships moving on the water in front of us. Marcella saw them, too.

"Ah! There are symbols for you, Len. Those ships coming in— their flags, colors, their very shapes are all symbols of the country they represent. Isn't that so?"

"Yup." This I could understand. "See that first one. A beauty. She's the *Conti di Savoia*. Italian. You're right about the colors. The red and green stripes on the two white funnels are the colors of Italy."

"There! What did I tell you! Symbolism!"

"The second ship is the German *Europa*. The third one is Japanese, *Shigamitsu Maru*. They come and go all the time."

"There is more symbolism here than you realize, Len. Those three ships collectively symbolize nastiness and evil. They symbolize trouble. I don't even want to look at them. I'd rather paint the rocks. The rocks are calling me. 'Paint us,' they say."

Marcella shifted her position, rearranged her paint box and water can, and began a new picture.

I watched with wonder as she quickly outlined a design with a hard pencil on a pad of heavy watercolor paper. It always amazed me to see a picture materialize out of nowhere on a blank sheet of paper. Watching photographic paper bloom with a photographed image in a darkroom was a magical experience. And it was just as magical for me to see a human being produce a picture with paint and brush on a blank sheet of paper. Marcella Marchand was a magician. That's how I saw her.

"Do you mind if I ask you a dumb question, Miss Marchand?"

"Ask away. But I hope you don't mind if I do not turn around. Once I get started I have to keep going."

"Why is it that you sit there, look at the rocks, and then work out a picture that doesn't seem at all what you looked at." I was persistent.

Marcella sighed. "I see that I haven't made myself clear. Look here," she responded with a noticeable impatient edge to her voice. "All that I am doing here is making some quick color sketches—not finished pictures. I am using the rocks inspirationally. I shall take these sketches back to my studio and use them to paint larger, more finished, more serious works based on this jetty. What's more, those paintings will be oils on canvas!"

"Do you think you will ever paint the ships and water out there, Miss Marchand?"

"I doubt it, Len. I doubt it very much. The ships come and go. There is nothing permanent about them. Not only do they disappear in front of your eyes as they sail in and out of the bay, they also have a habit of sinking or dying. That's what happens when a ship sinks. It dies. That lack of permanence does not interest me."

"Nothing lives forever, Miss Marchand."

"No, Len. Nothing but the constant struggle. That is immortal—the constant struggle. And that is why I have turned my attention to these rocks. The jetty symbolizes the constant struggle and the permanence of natural forces—of natural power. This jetty, Len, is the very essence of immortality. I, too, am the embodiment of a permanent struggle. The struggle to create visions and have them survive me. I suppose I am reaching for immortality. No matter. I am one with these rocks."

"What about the water. The sea? It comes and goes like the ships—in and out—the tides, you know—without disappearing. That's a permanent struggle."

"You're catching on now, Len. To me the sea is unreliable—untrustworthy. It is forever in motion assaulting the land. The sea is destructive in its timeless hunger to drown or swallow everything in its way. These rocks resist all that. They meet the challenge of the sea and refuse to be done in!"

"Someday the sea will destroy these rocks," I insisted,

echoing what the old geologist had told me.

"Perhaps. But right now this jetty symbolizes a kind of wonderful idealism, meeting all challenges and surviving forever. We have to learn to resist, too, like the jetty, in order to survive. Things are happening in the world today that make this important. It is this notion of the human spirit—and that's what I'm really talking about—the human spirit—that I associate with the character of the jetty. And so I am going to paint the jetty in my own way, as I see it, to communicate an important idea. It will not be the architecture of the rocks that I shall paint. No. It will be the not so easily discouraged spirit of us—of we humans, come what may."

"I think we had better go back, Miss Marchand. The tide is coming in and it is getting dark. I'll help you carry your stuff."

"This has been an interesting afternoon. I have discovered some ideas in these rocks. And I trust you have discovered a thing or two. You probably think I am half mad. That is my privilege. After all, I am an artist. We see things a bit differently than your average bank teller. But let me tell you, when I finish this painting, people will choose to see what they want to see or what they are able to see. There will be people who will see only rocks. Some will indeed see a jetty. Others will see color, pattern, shapes, and forms. And there will be those who will see nothing at all. Some will hate the painting, some will like it, and the rest won't care one way or the other. And you can bet that there will be some who will misinterpret what I had in mind and put on canvas because the only thing they are interested in is what they have on their minds and what they would put on canvas if they could. But we—you and I—will know differently. Won't we?"

"Yup."

1938 ————————

Sea Gate was a sovereign state so far as Jake Plaut was concerned. Jake was the owner of the newsstand at the West Thirty-seventh Street terminus of the rickety Coney Island–Stillwell Avenue Trolley Car Line. The line's right-of-way inclined or declined—depending on which direction you were riding—up to the BMT subway station at Stillwell Avenue or down from the station—through twenty-three blocks of weedy backyards. I always rode the trolley believing that it was an amusement park ride rather than legitimate transport to the subway.

Anyway, it would have been too imaginative a connection for Jake to have related the Sea Gate idea to the principalities of Monaco on the French Mediterranean or San Marino in the north of Italy. But he knew that Sea Gate was one of those rare places within the continental limits of the United States that required the nearest thing to a passport—a Sea Gate pass—to cross its entirely legal gate-controlled frontier. And he, Jake Plaut—Plaut, the self-proclaimed Prince of Peace—that's what the huge sign above the newsstand read, "Plaut, the Prince of Peace—did not have a pass. Plaut, the Prince of Peace, did not live in the gate nor did he have any influential friends inside. Plaut, the Prince of Peace, was persona non grata—unwanted."

More properly known as the Sea Gate Association, Inc., the community was once the beachside playground of millionaires. Around the turn of the century, several of these millionaires secured a land grant from the City of New York. The grant assured them of self-rule for the next ninety-nine years. Membership in the association was limited to landowners and homeowners, a living example of twentieth-century Hamiltonian democracy. Members automatically had a voice in the Sea Gate government. Living in Sea Gate did not void one's American citizenship. But being a permanent resident—an "all-year-rounder"—lessened one's dimension and narrowed one's national perspective and obligation.

While the government of Sea Gate did not have the right to maintain an army or fly its own flag, it did have the right to levy taxes, fix its own roads, collect its own garbage, and maintain its own unarmed uniformed police force. Also, it had the right to erect and patrol an impregnable iron fence across its landlocked border with Coney Island's West Thirty-seventh Street to keep out anyone it did not want in. And Jake Plaut was definitely one of "those."

The idea that he had been fingered as a persona non grata by the Sea Gate authorities overwhelmed him. After all, the authorities no longer represented the millionaires. They were all gone by 1938, ruined by the Great Depression. Not only that, their world famous New York Yacht Club, once located on Poplar Avenue in the northeast corner of the gate, was gone—mysteriously burned to the ground. Now it was a sandy, overgrown, brick-strewn baseball field known as the "yacht club."

The idea that he, Plaut, the Prince of Peace, was prohibited from entering that land of Oz—that land at the end of the yellow brick road—that land at the end of the yellow car trolley line—was more than he could bear.

"Whoever heard of a Prince of Peace called 'Plaut?' " was heard everywhere inside the gate.

"There was only one Prince of Peace. And we know who He is. And His name isn't Plaut."

"Keep the crazies out of here!" roared the members of the Sea Gate Association.

For his part, Plaut, the Prince of Peace, replaced the simple sign above his newsstand with a more elaborate proclamation:

PLAUT, THE PRINCE OF PEACE
Saver Son Messiah
Holy Avenger
Eternal Enemy of Lucifer
Scourge of Sodom

BUY
NY Times Daily News Sun
Mirror World-Telegram
Journal American
Life and *Look*
Candy

Jake was the image of all those things he proclaimed to be. He wore his hair long—well below his shoulder blades. Deep black and well combed, it was held in place by a snow-white headband. Jake was bearded, too, beaded, colorfully robed, and sandaled. He was richly tanned "from my many years on the desert," his description of the Coney Island Beach. No one could buy a

72

newspaper from him without getting a softly spoken comment on love, brotherhood, sisterhood, peace, sinning, and doomsday.

He took his tormentors in stride.

"Give us a miracle, Plaut!"

"Walk on water, Jake!"

"Part the sea, Moses!"

"I am not Moses."

Miracles were Plaut the Prince of Peace's chief worry. He never seemed to be able to produce one. He blamed his failure on his ancient mother who prayed all day long in the Twenty-third Street synagogue on Mermaid Avenue that he would do no such thing—perform a miracle.

"God, my Father, always listens to my mother," he confided to my own father, who bought his daily paper from Jake without hurling insults at him. "God, my Father," he whispered, "is henpecked. Women run the universe. Even my Father, King of the Heavens, cannot help me, his Son, the Prince of Peace, when it comes to women—that woman—my mother!"

"That's plain ridiculous," my father told him. "God is omnipotent! All powerful! All seeing! All knowing! He is the Lord! There is no other! And no woman can tell *Him* how to run things!" My father had gotten a few of his own things off his chest in the privacy of that conversation. If *my* mother had heard any of it, Dad would have gone without dinner.

"Listen, my son," Plaut intoned gently.

"I'm not your son!"

"There are a few things about God, my Father, that He does not want to get around. One of them is my mother. The other is that He is not so all powerful, all seeing, all knowing as He would want all the rest of us to believe."

73

"How's that?"

"I happen to know that God, my Father, cannot build a wall that He Himself cannot climb over. That He cannot sit in His own lap. Now! If He was so all powerful He could do those things! No! He's just like you and me in that respect. After all, aren't we made in His image?"

"Image maybe," my father responded. "In deeds maybe not!" My father was not about to quit. "You are raving, Plaut, just raving. None of it makes any sense. If God is your father as you insist, then He is a man like you and me. Only men can be fathers in case you didn't know. And if He is a man, then all of us are not made in His image. My wife and my mother and my grandmother, my sisters and sisters-in-law, and the daughters I wish I had and do not have are most assuredly not made in His image. Maybe He is a She or a He-She. My wife would sweep up the floor with you if you ever said God was a man. She happens to think that God is a woman. What do you think of that? And I'll tell you something else. The word "god" is just a title, not a name. Nobody knows God's name. Maybe it's Rosie."

"God made man in His image," Jake Plaut, the Prince of Peace, persisted. "Woman came later—from a spare rib. I eat spareribs!"

"Fairy tales, Plaut. All fairy tales written by someone who looked, talked, and behaved like you. Probably an ancient scribe—the only guy in the tent who could write—and sold newspapers like you."

Plaut, the Prince of Peace, smiled benignly. He would bide his time. He cupped his hands in front of his face after selling my father a newspaper and quietly prayed, "Dear Father who art in Heaven, this man Ben Fisher is a sinner and a blasphemer and a doubting Thomas. He is a leading citizen of that wicked place behind the fence—Sodom Sea Gate on-the-sea. Help me to help him see the light and the truth. Amen."

"What? Who's a sinner? Sodom Sea Gate on the what?" my father yelled.

"Ah, Benjamin, my son . . . ," Plaut, the Prince of Peace, whispered.

"I told you, Plaut, I am not your son. I am older than you."

Plaut, the Prince of Peace, went on unperturbed. "Sodom, Gomorrah, Admah, and Zeboiim were all evil places destroyed by my Father, God. You have heard of Abraham's nephew Lot and Lot's wife and the pillar of salt? Soon I shall come through your gate—into your Sodom—and save your lost soul and everyone else's before my Father adds you to his list."

"Listen, Plaut! You are talking nonsense." I don't know why my father kept the debate going. He was like that. Always arguing about anything—even growing cucumbers in our backyard. This was no different. "When Barcelona was bombed to smithereens last March—Barcelona, mind you—that marvelous city of the senses in Spain—that beautiful city of art and wonder—Barcelona, the very place that Columbus announced he had found India, only that it turned out to be America—when Barcelona was destroyed, who did it, God? He would not have dreamed of such a thing."

"Yes, God did it! It was part of His grand design to remake the world."

"Plaut, you are crazy," cried my father the pragmatist, who designed ships for the United States Navy. "The Germans did it, that's who! With airplanes, that's how! Don't you read you're own papers? Bah! What's the use. Sell papers, Plaut. That's the light and the truth. A free press. And stay the hell out of Sea Gate. It's no place for you. We are a peaceful, decent, quiet, law-abiding

75

people. Sea Gate doesn't need you. And you do not have a pass."

"Benjamin, my son. The Prince of Peace doesn't need a pass."

True to his word, Jake Plaut, the Prince of Peace, did finally enter Sea Gate without a pass the day after trying to make my father see the light. And he came not through one of the three landlocked barrier gates—Surf, Mermaid, or Neptune Avenue—not over, through, or around the forbidding iron fence that separated Sea Gate from Coney Island and the rest of the world—but by rowboat. My brother, Rich, and I spotted him at the same time as we were scampering off the jetty.

Summer had ended ten days before. It was fall although it still felt like a warm summer day this second Saturday in October. It was noontime and low tide. Rich and I were having our last fishing fling of the waning season without luck. Nothing was biting. They were all asleep, probably too tired from bucking the current and the dangling hooks all summer. There was a storm brewing. An instant stab of a jagged lightning bolt linked the darkening sky with the distant Jersey shore. The deep rumble of thunder, a rising wind, was enough of a message. The storm was moving fast. Black cumulonimbus clouds had reached Staten Island. The sky darkened above us. The sea began to run fast and noisy.

"We've got ourselves a thunderhead, Rich," I shouted. "We'd better vamoose before the ax drops. Let's move it."

A dull, thunderous groan rolled out of the murky sky and echoed toward the city. A low, foggy squall line that had been sitting on the Atlantic horizon all morning had decided to move. Now it was upon us at noon.

A shifty, incoming breeze suddenly became a fierce wind knocking the warm, heavy air from one side of the Lower Bay to the other. It marked the choppy sea, which had changed color from light blue to deep charcoal with churning, white-capped water that raced past the jetty. Small waves, cresting at two or three feet, began hammering the bulkheads at Fort Hamilton on the other side of Gravesend Bay drenching Brooklyn's Shore Road with fanlike sprays. A light rain was falling.

"Come on, Rich, keep moving," I urged. He had suddenly stopped about halfway and was peering into the windy gloom.

"There's someone out there, Len!" he shouted at me. "Look! Over there! Do you see him? There's a guy in a rowboat just past the bend."

"Yeah! I see him. He's trying to make it to the rocks."

"Go back! Go back!" Rich screamed at the approaching boat. "He's going to smash up and drown! Go back! Go back!"

"Forget it, Rich. He can't hear you. Hey, what's he doing? What's he holding up? He can't be crazy enough to hoist a sail in this wind."

"That's no sail," Rich bellowed as the rowboat was carried within a few yards of the jetty. "It's a sign! It says R-E-P—REPENT REPENT. You know who that is? It's Jake Plaut, the Prince of Peace!"

"What's he doing out there, the crazy fool?"

Plaut had seen us. He hung on to his windswept sign and nearly fell into the water as the waterlogged rowboat, barely afloat, was shoved by the racing tide onto the small, sheltered beach on the Gravesend Bay side of the jetty. The rain had become heavier, slanting inland as it was driven by the wind.

"Peace, my sons! Peace!" Plaut, the Prince of Peace, shouted above the wind and through the rain as we hurried toward him. "I bring you peace," he proclaimed ceremoniously as he stepped out of the rowboat holding aloft his sign, REPENT REPENT. A large blue crab scooted out of his way.

He seemed to be echoing something the whole world had heard over the radio a week before, that last day of September. Neville Chamberlain, the British prime minister, confidently had said upon returning to England from a meeting with that maniac Hitler, "I bring you peace for our time." He waved a sheet of paper instead of a sign. And he arrived in an airplane, not a rowboat.

For fifteen days Europe held its collective breath as Adolf Hitler raged about a small piece of Czechoslovakia—the Sudetenland— that he said belonged to Germany. He had said the same thing about Austria in March and took over the whole country with his goose-stepping troops. He told both Chamberlain and the French prime minister, Edouard Daladier, that he had no further territorial ambitions beyond this tiny piece of Czechoslovakia. No one but Germans lived there, anyway, he told them. Let me have that little piece and I shall not bother you anymore. Europe would be spared; there will be no war, Hitler promised. He went on to tell the Englishman and the Frenchman that Germany would then have all the room his crowded country would ever need. As their talks continued, a German army band serenaded them day in and day out with one tune, "*Deutschland Uber Alles,*" the German national anthem—Germany over all—everybody—the whole world.

Finally Chamberlain and Daladier gave Hitler the piece of Czechoslovakia he wanted. The Czechs themselves had nothing to say in the matter. And the German army band struck up "*Deutschland Uber Alles*" one more time—on the airport tarmac as Chamberlain and Daladier boarded their respective airplanes for the trip home.

"Peace for our time," Chamberlain proudly announced. Everybody heard it on the radio. That was a week ago. The next day,

German troops goose-stepped in the Sudetenland. Everybody heard that on the radio, too.

"Hitler isn't through," my father cautioned. "He took the Rhineland two years ago. Austria and a piece of Czechoslovakia this year. Next year he'll want all of Czechoslovakia. Then something else. More and more until someone has the guts to say no more. Peace in our time. I doubt it. Why don't you boys go fishing."

"I bring you peace," Plaut, the Prince of Peace, repeated as a clap of thunder fell on the jetty. "I have come to show you and the whole world the ways of righteousness and goodness—truth and light."

It was getting darker by the minute. Lightning struck something in the water not a mile from where we stood on the beach. The thunder that followed was earsplitting. The Prince of Peace kept talking but the noise of the rushing air, hissing sea, and roaring thunder gave him no sound. His lips moved. That was it.

Plaut gathered up his wet, wind-whipped robe and climbed onto the highest rock at the jetty's base. There he held up his sign: REPENT REPENT, and bawled, "Hear me! O ye sinful children of Sea Gate!"

Another bolt of lightning stabbed the object a mile out on the water. The Prince of Peace ignored it. Rich and I headed for the rusty seawall ladder and our front porch. Jake Plaut watched us scramble up the ladder.

"I've come to warn you," he shouted after us. This time the wind carried his voice in our direction and we could plainly hear him above the roar of the storm.

"Change your ways! Money! One-family houses! All evil! Change your ways! Open your gates to the humble, to the lowly, the starving, miserable people of Coney Island. Mend your ways or my Father will mend them for you!"

With that, Jake Plaut, the Prince of Peace, crawled out to the end of the jetty and planted his sign in a rocky crevice where it stood on its shaky pole resisting the wind and rain. Again, a bolt of lightning struck an object on the water silhouetting Plaut, the Prince of Peace, against its eerie flash.

A great crackling roll of thunder shattered the air and Plaut, the Prince of Peace, stretched out his arms and looked up with reverential thanks.

"Money? One-family house? Evil? Change our ways? He's crazy," I told Rich in the shelter of the porch where we could see Jake Plaut midway out on the rocks looking skyward with his arms outstretched.

"I get only a quarter a week allowance," Rich moaned. "And who else is supposed to live in your house but your family. Plaut's wasting his time out there. No one can hear him."

"I think we ought to get him, Rich, before he kills himself. The rain has stopped. It's getting lighter."

"Okay."

A couple of minutes later Rich and I were on the rocks with Plaut, the Prince of Peace.

"I think you'd better get off the jetty, Mr. Plaut, the tide's coming in. No one heard a word you said out here, you know. You're wasting your time."

"Wasting time? Never. Broad is the gate—your Surf Avenue gate—and broad is the way that leadeth to destruction. There shall be weeping and gnashing of teeth."

"Beware of false prophets," I shot back at him with the only biblical injunction "worth remembering" according to my father.

80

"A prophet is not without honor, save in his own country. Is this not my country, too?" Plaut, the Prince of Peace, wanted to know. "This land—this Sea Gate—this kingdom behind a fence?"

"Look, Mr. Plaut, we don't have a king. Only a president—the president of the Sea Gate Association."

"They be blind leaders of the blind. And if the blind leadeth the blind, both shall fall into the ditch," Plaut, the Prince of Peace, continued.

"Come on, Mr. Plaut! Get off the rocks. It's going to be high tide soon and you'll drown if you stay out here."

"Rocks! Tide! Hear me, the Prince of Peace. Whosoever heareth these sayings of mine, and doeth them, I will like him unto a wise man, which built his house upon a rock."

It started to rain again. The sky darkened once more. The storm had come back. A bolt of lightning ripped through the black clouds and hit a tall chimney on Hoffman Island. Thunder echoed around the bay like lead balls rolling around in a bass drum. The sea heaved and twisted, smashing into the jetty along its entire length. The rain returned with steadier purpose flattening the water. We were all soaking wet. It was dangerous to stay out there. Rich and I should never have left the safety of the porch to urge Plaut, the Prince of Peace, to get off the rocks. Plaut, the Prince of Peace, would not give in. He held on to the sign pole wedged securely in the rocks and leaned into us preaching louder than before.

"And the rain descended," he shrieked above the wind, continuing his recitation of the Gospel According to St. Matthew (7:25), "and the floods came, and the winds blew, and beat upon that house; and it fell not: for it was founded upon a rock."

A crackling streak of lightning slapped the finial on the

81

conically shaped roof of the Norton's Point Lighthouse. It turned the rain in its path to instant steam and saturated the jetty with its eerie white-hot light. It seemed as if a lost aircraft in a movie had dropped a white flare over the jetty. I imagined I could even hear the engines of the ghost plane that had flown off the silver screen into the sky above us. Plaut, the Prince of Peace, drenched from the sea and rain, was not surprised by the snapping electrical stream that came out of the angry sky.

"Sinners all!" he screamed at Sea Gate. "This is the beginning of the end! Repent! Repent!" His final plea was lost in a thunderous cannonade overhead. Convinced that the end was near for the little fenced-in community on Norton's Point for keeping him and Coney Island society out, Plaut crawled out to the end of the jetty to witness the final assault. He turned on the slippery, mossy rocks in time to see another lightning bolt slam into the top of the lighthouse.

"He that is not with me," he bellowed into the suddenly silent air—the wind and hiss had quit as if the noise had been terminally sucked through a straw in an empty soda glass—"is against me."

Now the rain let up and Plaut, the Prince of Peace, waited for the end. "Like Sodom and Gomorrah, Admah and Zeboiim—evil places all," he roared, "wiped from the good earth for their wickedness by God, my Father, so, too, shall that fate be yours—any second now—oh ye blasphemous children of Sea Gate!"

Nothing happened. Lightning danced in the sky. Thunder chased the streaking electricity with heavenly booms. The sea crashed everywhere and gave up its debris. But nothing happened. Plaut, the Prince of Peace, wiped the rain and stinging brine from his red eyes. He looked impatiently all around like a targeted deer smelling danger. The realities that had once occupied a small corner of his brain were now obliterated by the chemistry and violence of the storm. He, Jake Plaut, was not Jake Plaut. He was the Prince of Peace. He had brought the storm to Sea Gate. But Sea Gate resisted. It would not fall into the sea. Battered by God's thunderbolts, Sea Gate remained. How could that be? Impossible!

Soaked by the foamy spray of the sea as it spent itself against the jetty, the three of us—Rich, Plaut, the Prince of Peace, and I— hung on to dripping boulders to keep from being knocked into the bay. If it weren't for Plaut, the Prince of Peace, and our miscalculation of the storm's demise, Rich and I would have sat the whole thing out on our porch or at worst, inside. But there we were, dangerously marooned.

Plaut, the Prince of Peace, glared at the land beyond the seawall. The middle of the jetty, always its lowest point since the day it was constructed thirty-one years before, was awash and impassable. The beach itself was nearly submerged. Planks and chunks of driftwood were everywhere, coughed up by the rolling breakers. A couple of empty, oily life jackets bobbed up and down on the still boiling sea. Tin cans, bits of rusty machinery, barnacle-coated stones, and dead fish littered the water and beach. The sea was vomiting all it could not digest. Plaut the Prince of Peace's rowboat had been picked up by the surf and hurled against the seawall like a paper cup in a bathtub. There it drifted, shattered, along the seawall, hammered by the waves, filling with water and partially sunk. Finished. We were cut off. Plaut, the Prince of Peace, clung to his rock, mumbling, praying, wondering what accounted for his failure, while Rich and I tried to figure out how to get off the rocks without swimming.

"I am with you always. Even unto the end of the world," Plaut, the Prince of Peace, howled at the sky still hoping that the

cataclysmic destruction of Sea Gate—maybe the whole world—
was near.

The rain had stopped falling from the dark and twisting sky. The
air seemed clearer at sea level, but just at sea level. Lightning
continued to flicker around the bay while the jetty vibrated with
every clap of diminishing thunder.

Out of the corners of his smarting eyes and through the sopping
strings of hair that matted the front of his face, Plaut, the Prince
of Peace, watched the huge British liner *Queen Mary* work her
way down the bay toward the Atlantic Ocean.

Rich and I spotted her, too, realizing that if they were
sailing, the storm was passing. In four days she would be in Cobh,
Ireland, and Le Havre, France, before berthing at Southampton,
England, her home port. Plaut slipped and slid but kept his feet
as he inexplicably and vigorously waved at the fluttering Union
Jack.

"Peace for our time, brothers," he yelled. "Peace! Peace! May
God, my Father, be with you!"

Not far behind, the squat German liner, *Bremen*, trailed the
"Queen" out to sea. Plaut, the Prince of Peace, squinted at
the large bulky vessel, once the fastest ship afloat. It was not until
she came abreast of Hoffman Island did Plaut, the Prince of Peace,
recognize her. Standing out full in the breeze, not two miles from
where we were, whipped straight and even by the wind, was the
German national standard—a red flag with a black swastika clearly
silhouetted against a circle of white.

"All they that take to the sword shall perish with the sword,"
Plaut, the Prince of Peace, roared at the ship, shaking a belliger-
ent fist. He had changed his focus from Sea Gate to Germany. As
he stood shaking his fist, a lightning bolt popped out of the still

tormented sky and scorched the ship's mainmast in front of the bridge. A clap of thunder fell on the ship. Plaut, the Prince of Peace, sank back among the rocks, jolted by the power of his divinely inspired warning. He had summoned heaven's rage.

"I am who I say I am," he happily shouted to us from his pulpit on the rocks. "I have made a miracle come to pass! I have unsheathed heaven's sword and have flung it at mine enemies! God, my Father, has finally heard me!"

The *Bremen* continued to trail the *Queen Mary* toward the open sea undamaged by heaven's power. The bolt that struck her proved to be the last electrical stroke of the storm over the bay. There were a few weak rolls of thunder as the storm moved northeast toward New England. The sun broke through and bathed the jetty in a joyous light as a New York City Police launch cautiously approached the jetty to remove us to safety. My mother had called the police and the coast guard. She and my father had their eye on us the whole time from the living room window, frantic with worry. Apparently Dad had tried to come after us but was turned back by the smashing sea. We never saw him. No matter. It was all over now.

The launch dropped a small boat into the water. Inside were two cops wearing life jackets. They rowed the boat into the lee side of the jetty and gently nestled its bow between a couple of seaweed-strewn rocks. Plaut, the Prince of Peace, was the first into the boat. He went willingly, eagerly, exclaiming to the startled police-men, "My time is at hand!" And that, too, was from the Gospel According to St. Matthew (26:18). They rowed him ashore where he remained with one of the policemen. The other officer came back after Rich and me.

Plaut, the Prince of Peace, was never again seen on the jetty. Nor did he ever venture into Sea Gate. After a five-day stay in Kings County Hospital for psychiatric observation, Plaut, the Prince of Peace, returned to his newsstand at the trolley terminal on West Thirty-seventh Street, a seemingly happier man than he had been before.

"I gave you a miracle," he told his customers, all of whom had heard what had happened on the rocks. News traveled fast in those parts. They only smiled and shook their heads in pity. Plaut, the Prince of Peace, grew happier and happier in his grand delusion, which had now become his fixed-in-concrete persona. He had entered Sea Gate without a pass; and had personally urged God to whack a German ship, both of which provided ample proof in his mind that he was who he said he was, the Prince of Peace. Sooner or later the world would know what sort of being sold newspapers at the trolley terminal on West Thirty-seventh Street outside the "gate" in Coney Island.

Left behind the jetty, jammed deeply into a rocky crevice, and strangely undamaged was Plaut the Prince of Peace's sign: REPENT REPENT. Not even the heavy tides nor the icy waters could dislodge it or obliterate its message.

1939

Diana Grant, our next-door neighbor, scanned the distance with her binoculars searching the vacant horizon with endless interest. It had been like that since the beginning of August—Diana Grant standing in the windless oppression of ninety-degree heat, her binoculars steady in her hands and not a ship in sight.

Now August was nearly gone—not by the heat, however, which slowly undulated along the empty line between sky and sea. And there she was, on the end of the jetty, peering through the curtain of wavering heat that put the empty horizon out of focus.

"What are you looking at, Miss Grant?" I asked her. I couldn't stand it anymore. I had to know. I had my own binoculars and trained them on the same horizon. "There isn't much going on out there."

"I know," she said.

"I don't get it. Are you looking for something special?"

"You might say that I am."

"Like what? Maybe I can help."

"The past, Leonard, the past. That's what I am looking for. The past."

The past? Boy, that was strange! No one took Diana Grant lightly, especially me. I was an impressionable seventeen-year-old college sophomore, a little ahead of my time. And I knew all about Diana Grant.

Miss Grant, whose sharp good looks belied her fifty plus years, had been a newspaper woman. She had worked for the Associated Press before quitting to write a novel. Diana Grant had been around. She had seen the world as an international correspondent. She had worked in an area that permitted few women to enter. Her sex stood her apart from the rest of her erstwhile colleagues. It made her coverage of world events as historic as the events themselves. Diana Grant's aggressive presence in world trouble spots sometimes made more news than the trouble. Nevertheless, her incisive reporting from the capitals of the world was considered the best in the business by those who knew about such things—her fellow reporters—men who were slow to admit it, if they admitted publicly at all. She did have supporters among them, however. Not many, just enough to have assigned her here, there, and everywhere.

But now Diana Grant was home and uncommunicative, at work on a novel. She spent days on end at the end of the jetty, withdrawn, lost in her own unfathomable thoughts and experiences, almost unapproachable by longtime friends and neighbors.

Diana Grant had been in Budapest, Hungary, trying to cover an obscure story about Hungarian troops taking a slice of territory on their mountainous border with Czechoslovakia and the Russian Ukraine when Hitler occupied the rest of Czechoslovakia. She was rushed to Prague in time to see the Nazis parade in and complete their takeover.

That was in March. At the end of March, the Associated Press sent her to Spain to cover the end of the Spanish civil war and Europe's newest strong man Generalissimo Francisco Franco. In

May, a nasty border war broke out between the Russians and the Japanese in the northern Chinese province of Manchuria, now occupied by the Japanese and renamed Manchukuo. Twenty thousand soldiers and civilians died in that brief war. Diana refused to be assigned there. She quit her job with the Associated Press and went home to Sea Gate to write a book and enjoy the marvels of invention and ingenuity at the newly opened World's Fair in Flushing Meadows, Queens, New York.

"I have seen the future, Leonard, and I am frightened," she told me.

My concern for mankind's future was not as perceptive as Diana Grant's prediction. I wasn't exactly dense, either. Talk of war in Europe and elsewhere had become such routine conversation around the dinner table that it became part of the expected daily routine. A kind of gab triggered by newspapers and invisible radio commentators like Lowell Thomas, Elmer Davis, and H. V. Kaltenborn. "They"—the Europeans or Asians—didn't include us and, hopefully, never would.

It was just that there on the end of the rocks, in the silent August heat punctured only be the gentle, slapping sound of the lazy sea washing in and out of the jetty's crevices, I could not replace the joyful promise of everlasting life with the fearful explosions of instant death.

"People seem to have no vision anymore, Leonard," Diana Grant sighed. "They seem not to have any reach, or a view of the horizon. Civilization is a longtime proposition and humanity insists on making short-term demands on it. I have seen nations legally suffocate and murder other people for nothing better than tribal revenge or some individual's personal greed. We—all of us— have allowed a race of killers to breed among us because we have no collective imagination to dream beyond the horizon. I am tired of civilization. It has failed. What is missing is humanization. Have you any idea what I am trying to say, Leonard?"

"Honestly, no."

"Well, let me put it this way. Look around you. How pleasant it is here. How calm, unthreatening, and inviting. Life here on the end of these rocks is warm and good. Not a hint of catastrophe. At least not at this moment. You can sit here seemingly forever untouched by trouble. How delicious. How wonderful. Would you agree to that?"

"Sure. That's why I come out here, I guess."

"Okay. That is just about what this planet Earth is like. It is a beautiful, colorful, spectacular jewel in the sky full of interesting and exciting things to see and do. I'd go so far as to call our Mother Earth a 'miracle in the heavens.' Why it was put here is beyond you and me. The trouble we see and hear about day in and day out is not with the planet, however. The trouble is the people on it! We have never learned to leave each other alone. Ever since people organized themselves into communities with rules—that goes a long way back—thousands upon thousands of years ago—half the people have been busy shoving their rules down the throats of the other half of the population. This business of 'you live by my rules, or else' has become more dangerous than ever, if not altogether wearisome."

"I haven't really thought about anything like that," I replied. "No one is pushing and shoving me."

"Maybe so, Leonard. But they will. Sooner or later. Well, no matter." Diana Grant put her binoculars up to her eyes again and swept everything in her line of vision from the Narrows to the north, westward across Staten Island, and southward to the Atlantic Ocean horizon.

90

"I have seen my share of pushing and shoving," she remarked while peering through the glasses. "I do not want to see any more of it. And since I think the immediate future holds no promise for a peaceful life and that the scary future will be upon us soon, I have no other choice than to search for the past and for whatever goodness was there."

"How can you go backwards?" I demanded. "The past is gone, finished. The only place you can see it is in old photo albums."

"I know it sounds nutty, Leonard. But somewhere, beyond that horizon, is a gentler time, a little less noisy, a little less frightening, a little less demanding—an innocent time that reached for the future and got us. And we've messed up a lot of dreams. Here we are, you and I, on the end of the rocks with no further place to go."

"The past is gone," I insisted. "There has to be a future beyond these rocks. This isn't the end! You can always jump into the water and swim farther out."

"You have the reach of youth, my boy. And that is good. But you will discover that the past never quite dies. Only people die. The things they made and used are still with us. The past lives on in your photo albums, in your memories, in old movies, in the newsreels, on records, and in museums. The past can be seen. It can be heard. It can be touched. We live inside the past—in buildings made yesterday and before yesterday. The past is the only thing we know about. Sorry to say, we never seem to learn from it. We inherit the past and with a few modifications hand it over to the next generation. And in so doing each generation in its ignorance or arrogance—I haven't decided which—has made its presence nastier and nastier, bequeathing its brand of insensitivities to the next generation."

Gray shades of history flicked through Diana Grant's mind as she continued her visual survey. She spoke of the Algonquin tribes who were scattered throughout our region long before the Dutch and English decided to settle the area. She mentioned the Canarsees who roamed our beach. She ticked off all the explorers who sailed into this bay: Verrazano, Esteban Gomez, Henry Hudson, Hendrick Christiaensen, and Adrian Block.

Diana Grant looked across the water and caught Staten Island's Fort Wadsworth and Brooklyn's Fort Hamilton guarding the approaches to New York Harbor. I was sure that in her mind's eye she could see the tiny fleet of English ships sailing into Nieuw Amsterdam, the tiny Dutch colony on Manhattan's tip, and telling Peter Stuyvesant to surrender or else. Stuyvesant surrendered in a pitiful rage. It was not difficult for her to imagine—or me, for that matter—I knew some history, too—the British general, Sir William Howe, coming ashore at Gravesend Bay—practically where we stood—with thirty-two thousand redcoats and beginning the invasion of Brooklyn at the start of the American Revolution. But that was another August, one hundred and sixty-three years ago.

"Was there ever an innocent time?" Diana Grant suddenly wondered aloud.

I heard the question as I was trying to corner a small crab that darted out of a crack in a rock, escaping into a clump of damp seaweed. I had no ready answer for such mental mysteries. If Diana Grant could not find peace and solace at the end of the jetty, that was her affair. If she was intent on disturbing my peace and quiet, that was another matter. I would have to deal with that or go home. I watched the water heave around the jetty. The tide was beginning to rise. I thought about returning to college in the weeks ahead as the water surged up and over my dangling feet.

Diana Grant stored her binoculars in their felt-lined leather case. She stared at the hot and empty sea. There was a sense of expectation as she watched the vacant horizon. It was as if she knew that whatever it was she awaited would soon sail into view. I felt her edginess but could not define it.

"Is the horizon always so hazy, Leonard?"

"Usually. There are times it is a lot hazier out there than now. Actually, it is not as bad as it could be. It's getting close to September and in September it gets so clear out there you think you can see over and past the horizon—only you can't. The earth curves away from you, you know. But it can get crystal clear in September. Believe me."

"The jetty is a good place to see things from, isn't it?"

"Yup. I can't help feeling—and I have felt like this ever since I was small—I can't help feeling that I can watch the world whenever I want to. But tell me, Miss Grant. What are you really looking for out there? Is there someone you know coming in on a ship?"

"No, not exactly. Like I said, I am looking for the past—for a more innocent time, if that is at all possible—because I know that I am not going to like the future—the events that are sure to come sailing over that horizon. That's what I am busy writing about—a book about a more innocent time. A history book, if you want to call it that—a history of broken dreams and broken promises. I want to remember and put into words the good things that have been and came to naught before it is too late to remember anything. I thought if I came out here to the end of the rocks, I could be that much closer to the horizon where the past, present, and future seem to collide and dissolve into one haze. I thought if I came out here I might see the problem and the project a bit more clearly."

"Why not go out in a boat if you want to get closer to the horizon," I asked her, knowing what a foolish question it was.

"A boat would never do. You know that. The horizon will always be at the same distance from you. Besides. A boat moves. And I would feel as if I would forever be chasing an elusive target that would forever be moving away from me. No. This jetty is perfect. It is anchored to reality. It is solid. It doesn't move. I do not feel like I am chasing something I can never reach. Somehow or other, I feel that I can touch the horizon from here. And that is a good feeling."

"I think I know what you mean," I responded while noticing the outbound tilt of the tide pole. "The tide is coming in, Miss Grant. Maybe we had better get off."

I squinted again at the tide pole and caught some spots on the horizon. The unbroken hazy skyline was breached by three smoking specks that grew larger as they moved irresistibly toward the bay.

"Here comes your past or something," I said, calling Diana Grant's attention to the horizon.

She jerked her binoculars out of the case and focused on the objects that intruded upon the quietly rising tide of the calm sea.

"That 'something' out there is most definitely not the past. Take a look. See the future."

I adjusted my glasses to see three American warships come into view—two destroyers and a cruiser.

"Just a couple of cans and a cruiser," I told her. "That's all. They come and go all the time. In fact, they will probably anchor in Gravesend Bay. That's not much of the future, if you ask me."

"They are the future, Leonard. Mark my word."

I shook my head thinking how complicated Diana Grant made everything.

"It's time to go," I repeated.

Several shocking days later, I found Diana Grant at the end of the jetty again. The two destroyers and cruiser were anchored in Gravesend Bay about a mile from the traffic lanes along Shore Road. A red flag flew from the cruiser's mainmast. A single barge, escorted by several small powerboats, shuttled back and forth between the cruiser and Fort Lafayette, a munitions depot island off Fort Hamilton. The cruiser was taking on ammunition, a risky business in Gravesend Bay. The two destroyers were anchored to form a protective screen against the intrusion of other vessels. A small gunboat kept circling the cruiser to ward off curious pleasure boats.

A loudspeaker droned on like a broken record. "Now hear this. Now hear this. Keep your distance. Explosives being loaded. Explosives being loaded. Keep your distance."

Every so often the naval excitement was punctuated by a bugle call. We could see sailors running up and down the decks of the big ship while others seemed to lounge over the railings looking at the water.

"Well, Leonard. What do you think of the future now?" asked Diana Grant.

The world was three days into September. The heat of the summer lingered still with lazy serenity. A salty fragrance mixed with the strong aroma of honeysuckle floated on the casual breeze. The life-giving sun was high in the sky, hot and burning.

"Why did they do it?" I asked. "Why? Why did the Nazis invade Poland? What did the Poles ever do to them? Now France is in it. England is in it. And we're next, aren't we?"

"All I can say, my boy, is that the view from the end of the jetty is the nasty future, not the innocent past. The dream is over. We have got us a world war again. More people are going to die than you'll ever be able to count. I shall have to put off writing my history of broken dreams. There'll be no one left to read it. I am going back to work for the Associated Press. They called me this morning. Once a newspaperwoman, always a newspaperwoman, I suppose. I knew this mess was coming. All of us did. I did not think I could face it. And now I leave for London tomorrow. Can't let a good story get by me, can I?"

"I guess not," was all I could muster.

"I doubt if we shall see each other soon again, Leonard. Anyway, I had to take one last look at my horizon. I leave the horizon and the rocks to you. Keep dreaming. That's the stuff of life—of humanity. Be good. Be well."

I said nothing as I watched Diana Grant slowly, carefully make her way back along the jetty's ridge to the beach. She turned once before climbing the rusty seawall ladder and waved. I waved back.

In ten days I would return to college. Nothing would ever be as it had been. Not me. Not the world beyond the horizon. Certainly not my world as seen from the end of the jetty.

"The jetty will always be here," I mused to no one. "These old rocks will inherit the earth."